Learning by Heart

Ronder Thomas Young

Houghton Mifflin Company
Boston

Library of Congress Cataloging-in-Publication Data

Young, Ronder Thomas.
  Learning by heart / by Ronder Thomas Young.
    p.   cm.
  Summary: In the early 1960s, ten-year-old Rachel sees changes in
her family and her small Southern town as she tries to sort out how
she feels about her young black maid, racial prejudice, and her
responsibility for her own life.
  ISBN 0-395-65369-X
  [1. Southern States—Fiction.   2. Race relations—Fiction.
3. Afro-Americans—Fiction.   4. Family life—Fiction.]   I. Title.
PZ7.Y8767Le   1993   92-46887
[Fic]—dc20   CIP
                        AC

Printed in the United States of America

AGM   10 9 8 7 6 5 4 3 2

For my mama and daddy

One

"I don't want to move into the house." I knew it was just about the rudest thing I could have said to Miss Isabella Harris. If we didn't move away from the store and into the house, there wasn't any reason for her to be sitting here on a footstool and wrapping Mama's dishes in newspapers. It was as if I was telling her to go away.

"It's hard to leave a place you know." Her fingers moved always the same, like a machine. "Even if you're moving on to a better place."

"I like the store," I said.

She nodded. "Always something going on, I would imagine."

"Every once in a while, on Friday nights, Cecil B. plays records right here from the store, and you can hear it on WCOY."

"That's the radio station, is it?"

"Well, yes ma'am. You know. Cecil B.?"

She shook her head. "I don't find myself listening to the radio much."

1

I was sure she must have heard him and just not realized it. "Did you hear that man telling jokes, in that funny high voice, on Ed Sullivan last Sunday?" I laughed just thinking about it. "Cecil B. talks in that same voice sometimes."

"We don't own a television, so I don't often see the shows."

I didn't remember ever talking to anyone that didn't watch Ed Sullivan. She crumpled newspaper and pressed it between the stacks of wrapped plates. "Your Mama seems to think you'll be needing more space with the baby coming so soon."

"I guess so, Miss Isabella."

She stopped her hands and straightened up. "Well, now, Miss Rachel, you are happy about this baby's coming, aren't you?"

I picked up a plate and tried to wrap it like her. "We were going to have another baby, one time before, but it died, before it could even be born." The paper just popped off.

Miss Isabella took it from me and fixed it. She shook her head. "I don't think you have to worry about that this time." She was back at it, the wrapping and packing. She handed me a plate to try again. "I got a real good feeling about this baby."

"I do, too, really, but, you know, maybe it's better not to talk about it too much, not to jinx it."

"Well now, Miss Rachel, jinxes don't have anything to do with it, and, for that matter, neither do my feelings. All that matters is the Lord's will." She closed the flaps on the full box, pushed it away and started on another one. "But then maybe it's the Lord's will that I should have such a good feeling about this baby because I sure do feel it, Miss Rachel."

"Don't call me *Miss* Rachel."

"Well, then don't call me Miss Isabella."

"I have to." The paper popped off again. I was still wrapping one for every five of hers. "You're grown up."

"I'd like it fine if you just called me plain old Isabella."

"There's some kids up the road that's lived up north — what's that place? Dee . . . ummm — "

"Detroit?"

"That's right. Yes ma'am. You been there?"

She shook her head, folded the flaps on another box and started on the special dishes, gravy boats and the like. "I been to Harrisburg, Pennsylvania," she said. "But I never been to Detroit."

"Well, they say they never had to say 'Yes ma'am' or 'No ma'am,' no matter who they were talking to, not even in school. Or 'No sir' either."

"Mmmmm-hmmmmm."

"Mama said that's okay if that's how they do it up there."

Isabella opened the cupboard above the sink and started taking out glasses. "Uh-huh."

"Well, is it true?"

3

Isabella stopped, rested her hands in her lap and looked out the skinny window between the cupboard and sink. "You know," she said, "when I was a little girl, we lived way out in the country, and I was just ignorant. Me and my sisters and my brother, we were all just plain and completely ignorant." She started wrapping again, slowly, like she had to warm up. "And we all had it in our head that Yankees living up north were big, hairy, half-human creatures. With tails." She laughed. She had finished another box. "With tails!" Her voice dropped down low and serious again. "People up north are people, just like us."

"I know that."

"Well then, what are you asking me? Whether you have to say 'Yes ma'am' and 'No ma'am'?"

I nodded.

"Well, yes ma'am, you do." She stuck her head into the cupboard to make sure she hadn't missed anything. When she came out she was smiling. "Calling me just plain Isabella, that's a personal thing worked out between me and you. 'Yes ma'am' and 'No ma'am,' that's more of a habit, and it's one I don't think your Mama'd like you to get out of."

Isabella went down under the sink to pull more stuff out. I went through the screen door into the store and stood by the meat case, just looking. Mama and Daddy were up front boxing a big order. I slammed the door going back in, but they still didn't look. "It's not that I don't like the house," I told Miss Isabella. "It's just that I really like the store."

Isabella nodded.

"We have a commercial. On the radio."

Isabella nodded her head. She wore a small white hat, made of a sort of net, like those beauty-shop bonnets, except without the frills, and not near big enough to serve any real purpose. "Is that a hairnet?" I asked.

Isabella smiled. "No," she said. "My church requires women to cover their heads."

I nodded. "I'll be back in my room," I said.

Isabella smiled.

Altogether we only had these two rooms behind the store to live in, and all I had to myself was a little bed off the side of the dinette behind a white paper screen, but Mama always called it my room. I'd gotten into the habit of calling it that myself. I lay down and listened to Isabella's hymn singing. She started out with Grandma Graham's favorite, "Nearer My God to Thee," and then went through a whole list of other ones, humming some, singing others in a low whisper.

Mama had talked to a different woman every day for two weeks before deciding on Miss Isabella Harris. I'd looked them all over, and she was for sure the best one. Tall and nice and different.

The house was good, too. I'd been happy about it the first time I walked through it with Mama and Daddy. There were two bedrooms, a bathroom, a dining room and living room separated by glass doors, a kitchen and a screened back porch. I'd have a real room there.

Miss Isabella whispered good-bye to me from behind the screen, but I pretended to be asleep. After a while I really was.

It was almost dark when I finally got up and went into the store. I climbed up on my stool beside the meat market. Daddy was cutting chickens into parts and the radio was on, playing our commercial. "Fred's Family Mart. Best Meat and Produce in Town," Cecil B. said. "Open twenty-four hours, seven days a week, for your shopping convenience."

Daddy grinned at me. Mama thought the radio advertising probably wasn't necessary anymore, but Daddy got just as big a kick out of hearing it as I did. "You feel all right?"

"Yes sir," I said.

Mama was up front at the register. Wallets, bandannas, key chains and sunglasses dangled from clotheslines crisscrossed over her head. Jimmy the plumber pulled down a pair of sunglasses to go with his milk and bread. Mama bagged the bread and milk, and he hung the sunglasses on his overalls. "You come back now," Mama sang out. Her red hair lit up, the way it always did in the sun, like an angel's halo. She came back and leaned on the meat case. "How'd you and Miss Isabella get along?"

I pushed a clump of hair that had fallen out of my

ponytail behind my ear. "She said I didn't have to call her Miss Isabella." I got my hair from Daddy. I'd been told that was where Mama got hers, too. From her Daddy.

Mama's face went into thin, serious lines. "What do you plan to call her then?"

"Just plain Isabella."

Daddy came up beside me, drying his hands on his apron. Mama looked at him. Her expression didn't change.

"But she said she thought it was important that I keep up 'Yes ma'am' with her because it's a good habit."

"I should say so," Mama said.

"Just plain Isabella sounds fine to me," Daddy said, "long as it's okay with her, long as Rachel doesn't mean no disrespect."

Mama nodded. "I'd expected to go with someone older, but I just liked her the minute I saw her."

"How old is she again?" Daddy asked.

"Twenty-three."

Sounded pretty old to me.

The front screen slammed, and Mama hustled back up front.

"Daddy," I said. "How come we have to move into a house?"

He was icing down the mullet, not looking at me. "You're going to have the time of your life playing in that big old yard."

7

"But I'm going to miss the store."

"Store's not going anywhere," he said.

The thing was, nothing was changing for Mama and Daddy. They'd be working all the time at the store, just like always. What that house and Miss Isabella Harris meant was that I was being sent away. And while I knew it couldn't help it, that it wasn't even born yet, all the same, I knew it was the baby's fault.

Two

Miss Isabella came back the next week to help pack up some more boxes. We only had two rooms, but there were high shelves in the kitchen and the back room reaching all the way to the ceiling. They were all packed tight, but everything was kept in a particular order. "A small space," Mama always said, "is no excuse for clutter."

"I can't help today," I told Isabella. "It's my tenth birthday. We're going into town to have lunch with my Aunt Celeste."

"Well, that's a fine way to celebrate a birthday." Isabella was already folding back the flaps of the cardboard boxes. She was like Mama in that respect. Always moving.

Aunt Celeste and Mama and I went to the lunch counter at Woolworth's; they both got club sandwiches, but I got the full-blown turkey and dressing dinner with green beans and macaroni. For dessert we had chocolate sheet cake; the lady behind the counter stuck a candle in my piece and lit it.

The blouse Aunt Celeste gave me had red and black embroidery up and down the front and pearl snap buttons. I didn't have anything fancy enough to wear with it, and I probably never would, but it didn't matter. It was beautiful.

After Aunt Celeste went back to the florist shop to work, Mama and I were supposed to buy some school clothes. It was hot, though, and Mama's back hurt. I wasn't having fun either, so I didn't complain when we came back with only a three-pack of undershirts and a three-pack of panties. Mama sat on the couch and put her feet up on a chair. I got her a Coke. She took a sip and closed her eyes tight like she had a headache. "I can't believe it's August already."

Isabella nodded. "This summer has just flown by."

"Do you sew, Isabella?" Mama asked.

Isabella shook her head. "No ma'am. Not really."

"You make your uniforms, don't you?" Even though Isabella wasn't working for us regular yet, just coming by to pack up and help out, she wore green uniforms with white aprons. I'd heard Mama tell Daddy how she liked that.

Isabella shook her head. "No ma'am. I just add on the pinafore by hand." She moved her hand from her neck down to her waist. Isabella's dresses were different; there was a matched piece of cloth that covered the regular dress top. "I buy the basic uniforms."

"And so you just add that on, as a special touch?"

"My church requires it," Isabella said. "That a woman's clothing be . . . modest."

"And what church is that now?"

"The Mennonite church, ma'am."

Mama nodded. "Well, they look real nice, just like they were bought that way."

"It's simple. I never even been on a sewing machine."

Mama stood up and jingled her car keys. "Well, I got to find somebody to sew for Rachel. I just can't go those department store prices." She sighed. "I don't guess you'd want to learn to sew."

Isabella laughed. "Miss Bobbie, I'd love to learn, but I don't think you want Rachel to be going to school in my sewing lessons."

Mama laughed. "I guess not," she said. "I better go check on Fred. You can get tangled up in a hurry out there by yourself."

"Yes ma'am," Isabella said.

I laid my new underwear on top of a box full of clothes. "We can pack this up. I won't be needing it before school starts."

"What grade will you be in this time?"

"Fifth."

"You like school, do you?"

"Parts of it," I said. I was tired, too. I didn't like shopping any more than Mama.

"Which parts?"

"The reading parts," I said. Miss Isabella was all

11

right, but I wasn't in a talking mood. "I'm going to get something to drink." I whacked the screen door behind me and knew as soon as I did it that I should have asked her if she wanted something, too. I just went ahead and got my bottle of chocolate milk, though. She didn't seem like the type to hold things against you.

Mama and Daddy were tied up with customers, so I went on outside. The green-and-red gas pump was still out front, but Daddy had let it go dry. He said that once you started pumping gas, they wanted you to check the oil and change tires, but kerosene wasn't any trouble, and the coalyard was a gold mine. "People are going to keep warm," he said, "no matter what."

Miss Hattie came hobbling out of the store; Daddy followed her with a box of groceries. Miss Hattie lived in the big wooden house right behind the coalyard. Usually she came over two or three times a day, buying no more than a bag of sugar or a carton of eggs at a time. That was all she could carry, depending on the cane the way she did, but if she needed more than that at one time, Daddy would carry it home for her.

"You come on over when you're ready, honey-child," she said to me, "and we'll get you measured up."

Turned out Mama had been carrying on to Miss Hattie about department-store prices, and Miss Hattie had told her that she was a regular wizard on the sewing machine, that she had supported herself most of her life doing other people's sewing. "You go on over there and see what she needs to get started," Mama said.

I'd been in Miss Hattie's house more than anybody else's on the Hard Road because her two grandnieces, Jeannette and Tamara, were about my age and would come stay with her for whole month-long stretches. I played with them more than anybody else outside of school.

I stood with my arms stretched out between the framed pictures of President Kennedy and Jesus Christ while Miss Hattie measured me twelve different ways and wrote all the numbers on a little pad. The skin on her long gray fingers was thin as paper, and I worried they might crack or crumble or just plain fall apart with all the fast pinning and pulling and writing. "I didn't know you did sewing, Miss Hattie."

"Well, I don't guess I've done much work for white folks, not in a long while," Miss Hattie said. "But then you look as if you would wear things just about the same as all my little girls."

Someone knocked at the front door. Miss Hattie straightened out my shirt and nodded toward the door. "Get that for me, will you please?"

"Yes ma'am."

It was Isabella, sent by Mama to see how things were going.

"We're all finished for now," Miss Hattie said. "Will you be buying the patterns?"

"No ma'am," Isabella said. Miss Hattie waved at

the rocker beside her, and Isabella sat in it. I settled on the stool beside the sewing machine. "I reckon Miss Bobbie will want to do that."

Miss Hattie picked up a pattern envelope from her sewing table. "Well now, this is what she looks for, these measurements here on the back of the pattern. Compare it to this list I've made here. Be sure and tell her to go by the list and to just put those regular store sizes out of her mind. Might be the same, might not. It all depends."

"Yes ma'am."

"So now you're going to be working for Mr. Fred and Miss Bobbie?"

"Yes ma'am."

"They're good people."

"Yes ma'am."

I wanted to go. I kicked a little at the stool legs. Isabella's head shook slightly, in my direction, so I stopped.

"And you're married, are you?"

"No ma'am."

"Any children?"

"No ma'am."

Miss Hattie brightened and straightened up. "Well, good," she said. "And don't you be getting married to any of these boys down here, because every last one of them got northern stars in their eyes. They think they'll be making a better life, leaving their homes behind, making cars up in Detroit."

14

Isabella smiled.

"I'm quite serious, young lady." Miss Hattie leaned forward and rested on her cane. "They might send for you, they might send you money, but all the opportunities in the world won't make for home and family." Miss Hattie leaned back and let her cane rest against her knees. "You see my point."

"Yes ma'am," Isabella said. "I do."

Miss Hattie took my hand and folded the list of numbers into it. "Now you take care not to lose that list. You don't want me measuring you all over again, now do you?"

"No ma'am." I thought she might call me honey-child, but she didn't.

Isabella tried to stop her, but Miss Hattie pulled herself up and hobbled to the door with us. "I don't mean to go on so," she said, "but these young folks think if they miss home, all they got to do is come back down, but without them, home's just going to wither and die."

Miss Hattie stroked my hair and patted my back. "You pick out something pretty," she said. Miss Hattie was always nice as could be to me, but she was a lot more serious in her own house than she was in the store.

A week passed, and Mama still hadn't gotten around to buying the patterns Miss Hattie needed. I didn't mention it. I wasn't sure about this idea of homemade clothes. I wondered if Miss Hattie had made Tamara and Jeannette's clothes. I didn't remember them wearing anything all that nice.

The thing was, though, everyone expected you to wear a brand-new outfit on the first day of school. Even boys that every other day were stuck with hand-me-downs showed up in stiff jeans. It was always way too hot for corduroy or long sleeves, but kids still wore them just because they were new.

I didn't mention it because Grandma Graham had said it wasn't good to have too much on your mind when you were expecting a baby, and Mama was even busier than usual with us having to move everything into the house. I did have this red dress that I hadn't worn all that much. Mama had bought it last spring on sale. That would be just fine for the first day.

But then after I'd gone to the trouble to work that out, with just three days left before school started, Mama took up the subject with Miss Hattie again. She was in the store for a two-pound bag of sugar and a half-dozen eggs. "I could have her one dress ready," Miss Hattie said, "as long as you pick out a simple pattern."

"Now what does that mean exactly?" Mama asked.

"Something without the fancy details. No cuffs or collars to mess with. Maybe a jumper."

"A jumper," Mama said. "That would be nice."

"You get what you need and come on over, honey-child," Miss Hattie said. "I might be sitting out back, trying to catch a breeze, so you check."

"Yes ma'am," I said.

"You take care, Miss Hattie," Mama said. She went back to get her pocketbook and to tell Daddy that we were leaving. "I didn't think to ask her where was the best place to buy patterns."

"There's a big cloth store over next to the cotton mill," Daddy said. "Try that."

It was a big store. There were rolls of material everywhere, and in back they had these books of patterns laid out on counters. Mama didn't like it. "This is just plain confusing," she said. She didn't like the way the cloth was arranged. "You'd think they'd just have some of it prepackaged. You know, in convenient amounts." Then she found a straight, sleeveless shift pattern — Quick and Easy, it said — on a metal rack. "This is perfect," she said. "I could get you some of those turtlenecks I saw to wear under it. They had four or five different colors."

One of the ladies helped Mama figure out exactly how much material she needed, and once she had that information there was no stopping her. She picked up forest green, brown and red cotton bolts. She had a harder time with the corduroys. "You like this rust?" I nodded. She held it under my chin. "Looks good on you." She piled on that bolt, then added a tan one. "Good fall colors," she said.

"You want me to choose?"

Mama shook her head, had them cut a piece off every bolt and paid for everything. We were out of there in thirty minutes. In the car Mama said, "Don't you see, we just keep it simple, one basic pattern, but in such great colors it's still a completely different outfit every day."

I pulled the green out and looked at it next to the rust corduroy. She was probably right.

"And don't forget that white blouse with the Peter Pan collar. And the beige one. And I'll get you those turtlenecks."

When we got back to the store, Mama walked across the street with me to Miss Hattie's. She was out back, pushing herself back and forth in a rusty glider. I noticed how she had Daddy's coalyard to look out on and that was all. She pulled her glasses down her nose a bit and studied the pattern. "Honey, when I said simple, you really took me to heart, didn't you?"

Mama told her about the blouses with Peter Pan collars and turtlenecks.

"That's a fine idea," Miss Hattie said. "Sensible." We all decided to go with the forest green one first. It would go nice with the white blouse, and I already had that.

"You're all set," Mama said.

Three

Miss Tyler was young and tall and blond, and I'd hoped I might get her for fifth grade. I got Miss Evers, who was short with very curly, gray hair, instead. She did come in that first day wearing a serape she'd gotten on her trip to Mexico. That was interesting. Aunt Celeste had a boyfriend once who had been to Mexico.

Most of the kids were the same ones from the year before and sitting in the same old alphabetical order. Neal Jessup was behind me, just like always, and Caroline and Cynthia were one row over, Garrison and Garrity, one right behind the other, just like always. I watched Caroline ease Cynthia's arithmetic book to the edge of her desk until it fell on the floor. I saw it coming, but everybody else jumped. Cynthia jumped the highest. Caroline laughed. Miss Evers turned around — she'd been talking a long time with the principal at the door — but didn't say anything.

There was one unusual thing. Over on the last row, next to the windows, there was a new girl. Her

19

name was Callie Thompson, and she was colored.

When I started school in first grade, Tamara and Jeannette were staying with Miss Hattie. I'd heard them talk about school often enough, so when I went, I figured I'd see them there. I didn't see them, or any of the other kids from around the store. "Why weren't you in school?" I asked Jeannette.

"Don't say that," Jeannette whispered at me, looking around for Miss Hattie. "She'll be believing you."

"I didn't see you."

Tamara had laughed. "You're white, silly. We don't go to school with you."

"Colored people got their own schools," Jeannette said.

That was that. I hadn't wondered about it anymore until I saw Callie Thompson sitting over next to the windows, writing away in her notebook everything that Miss Evers said. At recess she sat up next to the wall, with the teachers. They usually shooed kids away, onto the playground, but they let Callie Thompson stay.

When it finally was time to go home, most of the kids lined up for the bus. Caroline and Cynthia walked home. They did that sometimes, when the weather was nice. They lived just across the road, back a couple of blocks on Chinaberry Lane; Caroline's blue-and-yellow house sat back in the corner of Chinaberry Lane and Azalea Court, and Cynthia's light green house with a fence was right next door.

Callie Thompson and I were the only ones, except for some first-graders, sitting out front on the bench, waiting to be picked up. "How come you don't ride the bus?" Callie Thompson said.

I shrugged. "My mama likes to pick me up in the car," I said. "Why don't you?"

"My mama's afraid there might be some trouble." She stood up and ran to the curb. Her mother had the car door opened and ready for Callie Thompson to jump right in. Mama pulled up right behind her.

"How was the first day?" Mama said.

"Fine."

"Chinaberry Lane," I said. "Don't you think that's a nice name?"

"Very nice," Isabella said. "Those chinaberry trees can make quite a mess in the summer, though."

"That's where Cynthia and Caroline live." I was lazing around on the floor while Isabella ironed. "I been over to visit them a few times."

She flicked water on the shirts with her fingers. "They're in your class at school, are they?"

"Yes ma'am." I laughed. "They live right next door to each other, and Caroline's birthday is on January twenty-fourth, and Cynthia's is the very next day, on January twenty-fifth."

Isabella buttoned the shirt on the hanger and smoothed down the front. "They must be like sisters." Isabella was always doing something when we were

21

talking, but even if she wasn't looking at me, I could tell she listened.

"They fight all the time." I sat up and looked out the front window. The lady across the street was sweeping her yard. "Wonder how they came up with an ugly name like Brown Street?"

Isabella set the iron up on its end and changed the setting for Mama's dress. "I'd think," she said, "it was the name of some important family, maybe the first ones that lived here before it even was a street." She picked up the iron and looked at me. "You know what I'd do? I'd go next door and ask Miss Peaks. You could even tell about it at school."

I lay back and closed my eyes. I didn't really want to know. Isabella flicked some of her water on me. "You go outside right now and look around at what you got on Brown Street." She smiled at me because I sat right up. "And you be grateful."

I did it. There was a pecan tree and an apple tree in the long backyard; it was fenced with chain link on the sides and ended in a tall hedge. "You could set four of these little houses in that yard," Daddy had said. "But that's the way I like it."

I looked straight out to the hedge, up into the branches of the big trees, into the cotton clouds. I hardly saw Daddy since we'd moved into the house, but he'd bought this place for me, just as much as for the baby, so I knew he loved me. I was grateful for that.

Miss Peaks's head ducked in and out of her kitchen

window. Her house was two stories, with a backyard full of flowers and trees. The Haynes place, on the other side, was brick and overgrown with twisted vines. It was right next to my bedroom window, and it was scary. On the other side of that was a white, peeling house with a FOR RENT sign stuck in its dirt yard.

Isabella ran down the back steps and grabbed my hand. "Come on!"

She let go of my hand and took off for the hedge smooth and strong and muscular, hitching the skirt of her uniform just the slightest bit. She touched the hedge and headed back.

She beat me. I fell out beside her on the grass. "You know what else?"

She shook her head. "No. What?"

"There's a colored girl named Callie Thompson in my class."

"Really?" Isabella was surprised, too.

"How come, do you think?"

"Why is she in your school, do you mean?"

"Yes ma'am."

Isabella looked out toward the hedge instead of at me. "Where you go to school has to do with where you live."

"No." I sat up and shook my head. "Everybody that lived around me at the store was colored, and they never came to my school."

Isabella stood up. "Well, there's white schools and colored schools, Rachel."

"Then how come Callie — ?"

"Well now, the actual law of the land, it says there don't have to be these separate schools, so people like Callie, they got the choice, in actual fact."

"Then I wonder why Jeannette and Tamara never came?"

Isabella opened the screen. "Maybe they just felt more at home in their own place." She went up onto the porch. "I need to check those collards."

It was almost time for Mama to come take Isabella home.

Isabella came back out. "Rachel?" she said.

"Yes ma'am?"

"Was there any trouble? With the little colored girl being there?"

The only trouble we'd had was Caroline messing with Cynthia, and then Miss Evers running out of science books with two kids left. I shook my head. "No ma'am."

Isabella nodded. "Maybe folks won't take much notice of just one little girl."

"Sure smells good in here!" Mama had come in the front door and was in the kitchen.

I didn't know about other folks, but I sure took notice of Callie Thompson. I liked her hair. Her ponytail stuck up higher than anyone else's, and it somehow stayed perfect all day long. My hair was a scraggly mess by lunch.

* * *

24

After Mama drove Isabella home, she went to the store
and sent me to Miss Hattie's house to pick up the rest
of my shifts. There they were, the brown, red, rust and
tan ones, not looking any different than the forest
green one and not much different than the plain cloth
had looked. It wasn't Miss Hattie's fault, though; they
looked just like the Quick and Easy picture on the pattern.

"Miss Hattie?" I said.

"Yes?"

"When are Tamara and Jeannette coming back?"
Ever since Buddy went to Detroit — Buddy was Miss
Hattie's nephew and Tamara and Jeannette's daddy
— they stayed with Miss Hattie as much as they did
with their own mama.

Miss Hattie shook her head. "They're up north
with their daddy now."

"How come?"

"They're teenagers." She smoothed my hair down
in back, but looked straight ahead, at something else.
"More than me or their mama can handle."

"But they'll come back? To visit?"

"Oh, they'll all be coming back." She closed her
eyes and shook her head. "But to what?" She opened
her eyes, but she still didn't turn them back to me.

"Well," I said. "Tell them I said hello." I paid her
the fifteen dollars we owed her for the dresses.

"I do hope you enjoy them," Miss Hattie said.

"Good-bye, Miss Hattie," I said. "Thank you."

Four

The baby was born in October, and it was a boy. They named him Jesse. I waited by the window for him to come home from the hospital. Grandma Graham sat behind me rocking, drinking tea and grumbling. "Just sit yourself down, Rachel. You make me nervous dancing around like that." She folded her arms and leaned back. "I don't know what you expect from this baby. All they do is sleep."

Isabella called me into the kitchen, where she was fixing dinner. She leaned down and whispered that it would be okay to wait on the steps as long as I put on my jacket. It was overcast and drizzly, but not really raining. I went out the back door and around the house so I wouldn't have to pass Grandma.

A taxicab pulled up in front, and the people across the street came out on their porch to stare. It was only Aunt Celeste. "Carter was supposed to come by for me, but you know how slow he is," she called up to me. "Are they here yet?" I shook my head, but Aunt Celeste wasn't looking. She counted out money into the driver's hand, then ran up to sit beside me.

"Don't taxicabs cost a lot of money?"

She shrugged. "We don't get a new baby every day." She poked around the back of her head. "Is it falling down back there?" It was high and fancy, in a French twist.

"No," I said. "It looks good."

She looked over her shoulder. "Your grandma in there?"

I nodded.

"Well, just don't mention that taxi thing to her."

Then Mama and Daddy pulled into the driveway in the old pickup. Daddy got out, holding Mama's blue overnight bag and agreeing with her that he should have brought the car, that he just wasn't thinking. Aunt Celeste held out her arms, but Mama hugged me first, with little Jesse right in between, and, I tell you, no doll could ever get you ready for how sweet and soft a baby feels.

"Watch out!" Grandma Graham yelled from the stoop. "You'll squeeze the life out of the little thing." Daddy helped Mama up the steps, and Grandma waited there to snatch the baby away from Mama.

"I need to lie down," Mama said.

Uncle Carter brought Great-uncle Hewitt over from the nursing home. "He's the best one this family's seen yet." That's what Great-uncle Hewitt had to say about the baby. Now Great-uncle Hewitt had patted me on the head any number of times and said, "Every bit as good as a boy, this one, Bobbie," and right up until then that had made me feel special. All of a sudden it made me feel mad.

Aunt Celeste and Uncle Carter whispered to Mama, coming at her from different sides. When Mama's people were in a room together there was always a lot of whispering.

Daddy edged out the bedroom door. These were all Mama's people. There wasn't anybody on Daddy's side. "Dead," was all he'd say about his family, "or good as dead."

Mama watched him. Her face was white as the pillow it lay against. "Honey, why don't you drive Mama home."

"No," Grandma said. "I aim to stay where I'm needed."

Daddy put his hand on Grandma Graham's shoulder and led her out of the room. "Now you go home and get a good night's rest in your own bed. Isabella'll stay a little later tonight."

Aunt Celeste left with Uncle Carter, arguing all the way out to the car about why she couldn't have a little patience. "I went all out of my way for nothing," he said. Great-uncle Hewitt shuffled out behind them, shaking his head and smiling at something.

The house went quiet again, Mama rolled over and

closed her eyes. I stood over the bassinet, watching Jesse sleep, with his little backside stuck up in the air.

Right before Mama went into the hospital Daddy took to closing the store at midnight and opening up again at six in the morning. The new WCOY commercial sounded almost as good — "Open six to midnight, seven days a week" — but I didn't get as big a kick out of hearing it as I used to.

Seeing Daddy meant getting up early or staying up late. On school nights I couldn't get out of bed, but I got into the habit of waking up and listening. Daddy sat at the table eating whatever was left over from dinner and talked things over with Mama. She worried over everything, but mostly about what kind of instructions to give Isabella. "I never had any dealings with a maid before," Mama said. "I don't know how to set things up."

"Just let nature take its course."

I could see Mama roll her eyes even though she was in another room. Daddy would say that in answer to just about anything, but it always made sense to me. "What's that mean?" she said.

"Just don't worry about how other folks do things," Daddy said. "Just worry about what it is that has to be done."

Mama settled first on having dinner ready at five, but that was kind of crazy since Daddy couldn't get away then, and we had to rush to eat before she took

Isabella home at six. Mostly dinner was just put away and heated up later. Then she hit on the idea of dinner being ready when I came home from school. Other people might not do it that way, Mama told Isabella, but I was always hungry after school, and a plateful of vegetables made more sense than filling up on cookies and milk.

Isabella said she thought it made a lot of sense. Most days Mama could take time to eat, then take a hot plate back to the store for Daddy. When she couldn't come in and eat, Isabella and me ate sitting on two stools at the kitchen bar. When Mama was there we set the dining room table. The first time Isabella kept her plate in the kitchen, and she and Mama shouted back and forth through the door.

"Did you try that new cleaner? Do you think it's any better?" Mama said.

"Yes ma'am, Miss Bobbie. Did you see those tiles on the porch?"

"Oh yes!"

They were getting on my nerves.

"Did you cook the okra in the oven or on top?"

"In the oven," Isabella said.

"I like it."

I had one of my after-school headaches.

"Isabella?"

"Yes ma'am?"

"Come in here and sit down with us. I'm getting a stomachache yelling like this."

Isabella brought her plate and tea to the table. "You sure, Miss Bobbie?"

"That's the usual way, I guess. With you eating in the kitchen?"

Isabella nodded.

Mama sighed. "Well, I'm too busy for all that. I don't have any other time to talk to you." She took a bite of cornbread. "You use buttermilk in this?"

"No ma'am. Sweet milk."

"Try the buttermilk next time. It makes a world of difference."

We went through the same thing in the car. When Mama took Isabella home, we both went for the backseat. "I'm not being a chauffeur," Mama said.

"I want to sit in the back."

"Why?"

"Because you keep looking in the backseat to talk to Isabella, and I'm afraid we'll be killed."

Mama laughed. She raised her eyebrows at Isabella.

Isabella shook her head at me and sat in the front seat.

All that stuff was settled by the time Jesse was born, but the ten days Mama stayed home from the store threw everything else out of whack. I wouldn't tell anybody this, but when she went back to work after those ten days, I didn't mind. It was only then that I was able to really poke around and get comfortable with Jesse.

Five

I spent most of my Saturday morning sitting outside in the corner nearest the Haynes place. Yellow and orange chrysanthemums had opened up and pushed through their vines. A pickup truck with two blond kids and a little baby pulled up in front of the white house. I watched them take out a mattress and a playpen and a table and two chairs. I grimaced when the baby fell down and scraped her forehead. When Isabella came out with Jesse, I said, "There's people moving into the white house."

Isabella only worked half days on Saturdays, so she scooted me on in to wash up before Mama got there. She stood and watched the kids herself, though, until that baby stopped its crying. Mama was late. She came hurrying into the house about one-thirty. "Isabella, I'm so sorry. I got hung up."

"That's all right, Miss Bobbie." We were sitting on the living room floor, dancing a stuffed bunny and a bear back and forth to Jesse. He was on a blanket, on his tummy.

Mama scooped Jesse up, gave him a kiss, then put him back on the floor. He didn't mind. He was the most contented baby you'd ever want to meet. "I hate to ask you, but could you just help me do one quick thing?"

"Sure, Miss Bobbie." She followed Mama back to the little space behind the dining room. When we'd first walked through the house, I'd asked Mama what that room was called; she said you called it whatever you needed at the time. Since Jesse, it had been the nursery.

"Just help me pull this crib back into our room." Mama pulled on the crib. The wheels squeaked.

"Miss Bobbie, we're going to have to pick this up. It'll ruin the floors."

"You think so?"

Isabella nodded. They both lifted the crib and went a little way. This took longer than just pulling because Mama stopped every couple of feet and got a better grip. I'd felt Isabella's muscles; they were hard. Mama didn't have any I could see.

Even though Mama'd already wasted a half hour of Isabella's time, she didn't pull right out of the driveway. We were all ready, in the car, with the doors closed, and she just lay her head down on the steering wheel.

"Something wrong, Miss Bobbie?" Isabella said.

Mama sat up and sighed. "There might be a surprise here on Monday, Isabella. My mama might be here . . . to stay for a while."

I felt sick to my stomach.

"Yes ma'am?"

"Well, just bear with us, okay? It won't be forever." Mama started the car and backed down the driveway. Once we were on our way she said, "The thing is, I have to take what she dishes out because she's my mama, because I know what a hard time she's had, but you don't. Lord knows, I want you to be respectful as you can — Lord knows, you would be — but I don't want you to take anything you shouldn't have to take." Mama looked at Isabella. "You know what I mean?"

"Yes ma'am."

When she pulled in front of Isabella's she leaned over and whispered, "And help keep Rachel from getting in her way." I heard her.

"Yes ma'am." Isabella turned around and smiled at me and Jesse.

Isabella's brother stood on the porch, looking mean. Isabella didn't mind being a little late, but he did. Mama waved. He didn't wave back.

"I thought Isabella said he was a preacher," Mama said as we pulled away.

"He is."

34

"Well, you'd expect a pleasanter disposition from a preacher."

Grandma Graham lived with Uncle Carter at the old homeplace. It was actually more correct to say that Uncle Carter, Mama's brother, lived with Grandma, since it was the house where she'd lived as a child, and then she came back when Mama and Celeste were children. Mama, Aunt Celeste and Uncle Carter, they had all grown up there, but Uncle Carter had just never left.

Uncle Carter was thirty-six years old. I never thought about or cared about how old anyone was, except maybe whether a kid was eight or nine or in the third or fourth grade, but with Uncle Carter I always knew. Mama or Daddy would say, "You'd think he was three, not thirty-three" or "Well, he's thirty-four years old, what you going to say?" or "Thirty-five years old and still sneaking around behind his mother's back." Uncle Carter wasn't married and usually never had a girlfriend for very long; sometimes he'd bring them by the store to meet us, but on the way out he'd whisper to everybody, "Don't mention this to Mama."

"Thirty-six years old," Mama would shake her head and say, "and he can't even take a girl home."

But now Uncle Carter had a girlfriend — Miss Macy Mitchell — who had insisted on meeting

Grandma Graham. "Mama didn't scare this one off," Mama told Daddy, so the day after she warned Isabella it might happen, Grandma came to live with us. A rollaway bed was pushed into that space off the dining room. Then we called it Grandma's room.

Grandma sat at the dining table and looked blankly around the room. "I hope you don't forsake your parents when you're all grown up and able to take care of yourself."

I was at the table drawing. I looked up, but Mama said, "I think you'd be hard-pressed to find a more devoted son than Carter, Mama."

"Hmmmph."

"And that Macy, she's a good-hearted girl."

"You don't know, you don't know what I've heard."

Mama gave up. She helped Grandma move a chair underneath the phone in the kitchen and dialed Aunt Celeste's number. "Celeste, call your brother and have him move the old churn and the silver punch bowl out onto the side porch." She looked around. Mama raised her eyebrows and held up a teacup. Grandma shook her head. Mama held up the Kleenex. She nodded, and Mama set the box beside her. Grandma took one and dabbed at her eyes and lips. "Is that too much to ask? I've been thrown out of my house — "

Mama rolled her eyes.

"Well, I don't know what you've heard," Grandma

said into the phone, "but Bobbie's taking me over tomorrow to pick up my things."

Aunt Celeste, of course, finally agreed, and Grandma hung up, smiling. The phone rang right away.

Mama answered. "Mama, it's Carter."

Grandma stared at the wall. "I don't have anything to say. Tell him Celeste will be calling him."

Mama hung up and put Jesse down for his nap. "Mama, I think I'll run down to the store and help Fred out a bit while Jesse's sleeping. Rachel can help you with anything you need."

I sighed.

"Can I bring you anything, Mama?"

"Don't get anything special for me."

"You sure?"

"Well, some strawberry ice cream would be nice." Grandma stood up and tried to move her chair back to the table. Mama took it from her. "And a few bananas."

"No problem. I'll be back soon." She winked at me. "There's a stack of clean diapers on our bed, Rachel, but you probably won't need them." She almost ran out the door. Grownups do whatever they want whenever they want.

Mama dropped me off the next day after school. She didn't have time to come in and eat. Dinner wasn't ready yet anyway. Grandma was standing beside Isabella, coming right about to her shoulder, pressing her finger on the dough rolled out on the counter. "Too much shortening," Grandma said. "You want me to show you how to do it right?"

"Yes ma'am." Isabella stepped back.

Grandma stepped up, pulled up the dough and threw it in the trash can. "You chop up those onions and carrots."

"Yes ma'am."

Grandma's chicken pot pie was very good. Isabella said it was wonderful. She ate hers in the kitchen. The next day Grandma made meat loaf — she mixed the mixture with a meat fork, not her hands, to keep it tender — and Isabella peeled the potatoes. The next day she cooked chicken while Isabella scrubbed the toilet. One night I heard her on the phone to Aunt Celeste saying, "Here Bobbie is with a maid that doesn't even know how to cook."

I stared at her. I let her know I'd heard her. I wanted her to know I hated her.

Grandma looked at me and said, "There's more of that fruit salad left in the refrigerator. You going to have a bowl before bed?"

"Yes ma'am," I said.

The next Sunday Grandma Graham made her chicken pot pie again. Great-uncle Hewitt was coming to our house for dinner. Great-uncle Hewitt had lived at the old homeplace with Grandma Graham and Uncle

Carter until two years ago, until he got so old and feeble that they had to move him into the nursing home.

Usually Uncle Carter picked him up and helped him up the front steps, but Grandma and Uncle Carter were still on the outs, so Mama had to do it all herself. She sat him down in a rocker in the living room and dialed Daddy at the store. Daddy told Great-uncle Hewitt he expected him to come over to the store and just sit around and shoot the breeze. Great-uncle Hewitt leaned on his cane, even when he was sitting. "I just might," he said. "I just might do that." He used to do that every Sunday, but it was plain to see he wasn't ever going to be able to do it again.

Instead of serving our own plates from serving bowls on the table, Grandma filled our plates in the kitchen. When I went in to get Great-uncle Hewitt more ice, I saw the pot pie dish was completely empty. I looked in the refrigerator and saw Grandma'd already put it away.

"Can I get you anything else, Uncle Hewitt?" Mama asked.

"I'd love a little more pie." His leaning made me nervous. "Ginnie knows it's my favorite."

"There isn't any more." Grandma collected our plates. "We can have dessert."

Mama was shocked. "There has to be more."

Grandma took the plates into the kitchen and came back out with three bowls of banana pudding. "Now you can't have any of this."

Mama said nothing. Great-uncle Hewitt sank deeper into his chair.

Grandma sat down and picked up her spoon. She looked at them both. She looked confused. "They told me at the home. No sweets. You heard them, Bobbie."

Mama pushed her pudding to me. "Take this, and yours, into the kitchen." She stood up and helped Great-uncle Hewitt into the living room. "Would you like to listen to the radio?" She fiddled with the dials until she found a band program he liked.

I set our pudding on the counter and slid out behind Grandma sitting alone at the dining room table, scraping the sides of her bowl. I loved banana pudding, but I was afraid to even taste it. I went into my room and closed the door.

"Rachel?" Mama knocked on the door after about twenty minutes.

"Yes ma'am?"

She opened the door. "I'm taking Uncle Hewitt back. You want to go?"

I shook my head.

Mama was holding Jesse. He waved his hand around and poked her in the nose. "Well, I'm taking Jesse. Macy's working tonight." Macy Mitchell was an attendant at the nursing home. That's where Uncle Carter had met her. "Sure you don't want to go?"

I nodded.

"Well, come on out and say good-bye."

I hugged him. He wasn't big and solid like he used

to be. He was loose. I walked out to the car holding his arm.

"You come back, Hewitt, just as soon as they let you," Grandma said from the porch.

Great-uncle Hewitt nodded.

"I want to show you something Rachel," Grandma said when I came back. She put her hand on my shoulder. Grandma didn't touch me much.

"Okay."

I sat on her bed in her little room for the first time. The churn was tucked in at one end of the bed and the silver punch bowl at the other. Grandma pulled her family Bible from underneath the bed. She pointed out where her mother had entered Great-uncle Hewitt's name and birth date, then moved her finger down to her own name and date. "Didn't she have a beautiful handwriting?" Grandma said. She turned the page and showed me Mama and Aunt Celeste.

"You write pretty, too," I said. Jesse and I were on the next page.

"This is a treasure," Grandma said.

I woke up that night when Daddy came home from work, and they let me stay up even though there was school the next day. Mama, Daddy and I all sat around in the kitchen and ate the banana pudding.

Arrangements were made to bring Great-uncle Hewitt out again the following Sunday, but on Friday there was a phone call. Isabella took it. "Miss Ginnie, it's for you."

Grandma took the phone and looked at Isabella funny because she didn't move away. She just stood there, beside Grandma. "What?" Grandma said. She dropped the receiver.

Isabella took her arm in one hand and pulled up the receiver with her other. "It's all right," she said into the phone. "I'm with her."

Grandma cried and shook and reached up to Isabella. I just watched. Isabella helped her over to her bed and sat with her arm on her shoulders. Grandma leaned into her. "I had it all planned," she said. "I was going to let him eat all the pie he wanted. I was going to have Celeste bring over some of my canned peaches — he could have eaten those." She held her head down and cried some more. "I just wanted him to see how it felt, being lorded over, being told what to do."

Great-uncle Hewitt was dead.

Six

Everyone was touching. Aunt Celeste rubbed my cheek with the back of her hand. Grandma held Aunt Celeste's other hand. Mama kissed Jesse and squeezed Isabella's arm. I was held close on Isabella's other side. No one was talking. I didn't feel good, but I knew I didn't feel near bad enough. Great-uncle Hewitt was dead.

Mama had cried, too, when Great-uncle Hewitt had gone into the nursing home, even though she said out loud that it was for the best. I hadn't worried about feeling bad enough then because he still came over for dinner and I could still visit him and bring him boxes of Old Spice talc.

"It's getting late," Mama said. "I need to take Isabella home."

"No, Miss Bobbie," Isabella said. "I'm taking the bus tonight."

"No," Mama said. "Not in the dark."

There was a story about Mama and buses. Something about getting off and being chased by a stranger and losing her shoes. I never quite understood what happened, but I knew that was why she was so funny about buses.

"Miss Bobbie, I think — "

Mama shook her head. She kissed Grandma. "We'll be right back."

I settled into the backseat of the car with Jesse and closed my eyes. Great-uncle Hewitt used to bring me strips of multicolored lollipops as tall as myself. He used to say, "Every bit as good as a boy." I squeezed Jesse's little hand. I'd forgiven him for that. I felt as if Great-uncle Hewitt had been gone for a long time before he was dead, and I knew that wasn't the right way to feel.

"After the divorce," Mama said, "we all went back to the old homeplace. Celeste was just a baby, not even a year old. Divorce was more than a disgrace, it just was not heard of."

"Yes ma'am." Isabella's head was bowed. Her hands were folded in her lap.

"Mama cooked and cleaned and farmed, and, of course, by all rights, it was her home, too, but we were a disgrace." Mama wiped her eyes. "He did right by us, Uncle Hewitt, but you always felt, I know Mama did, if things had been done right, our daddy wouldn't have run out on us."

44

"She really did love Mr. Hewitt. You can tell that."

Mama stopped the car in front of Isabella's. "Thank you for putting up with us."

Isabella reached over and touched Mama's arm. "Yes ma'am." She sat there until her brother pushed open the screen door. "I'll try to get in a little early."

Mama shook her head. She didn't say one word to me and Jesse on the ride back. Uncle Carter was in the living room now, with Macy Mitchell sitting in a chair right beside Grandma Graham. Macy Mitchell wore stretched-out red shoes. Her feet and her face were wide and flat, but her hair was thick and black and wonderful. She talked to Grandma in a low, careful voice, and I guess Grandma was thinking about too many other things to mind.

The next morning I woke up real early. Daddy hadn't even left for work yet. I heard him say, "She just up and left with Carter?"

"Not just Carter," Mama said. "You should have heard that Macy, Fred, talking Mama out of her crying, talking about how they had to pick out the burial clothes and all. They left here the best of friends."

"I guess Macy gets a lot of practice dealing with contrariness in that nursing home," Daddy said.

I got out of bed and went out into the hall. Mama poured another cup of coffee. "I never knew Uncle Hewitt to have more than one old suit. They're probably going to have to buy something new."

Daddy slumped in surprise. "Bobbie, that's plain crazy, buying clothes for a dead man."

Mama looked at him. "It's going to be an open casket, Fred."

Daddy saw me and held out his arms. "A lot of coming and going, huh, squirt?"

I shrugged.

"Bobbie, bring her by the store after school today," Daddy said. "I've got a present for you, Rachel."

"What?" I said.

He shook his head. "Just a little something I took in pawn." He brushed the crumbs off his shirt and stood up. "I got to get on to the store." He roughed up my hair. "Why don't you go back to bed. No need to be up this early unless you have to."

"What is it?"

Mama shrugged. "I have no idea."

I didn't think I would, but I did go back to sleep, so I ended up being rushed for school. When I came out of the bathroom, Isabella stood at my window peeking through the blinds. "What are you looking at?" I asked her.

She didn't say anything, so I watched with her. The new people were in their yard. The girl was behind the steering wheel of the truck yelling at the boy. The boy pulled her arm with one hand and hung onto the baby with the other one. The girl gave him a sharp kick and closed the door. She screeched out of the yard with him waving his fist after her. The baby screamed.

Isabella let go the blinds. She stared at the ceiling for a moment before heading back into the kitchen.

"Boy oh boy," I said.

"Let's go!" Mama said.

If I wasn't going to be thinking about school, I should have been thinking about Uncle Hewitt and his life, but instead I was thinking about those people with the baby in the white house. It just came to me, all of sudden, during geography, that those two blond teenagers, they were the baby's mama and daddy. Before that I'd just thought of them as a couple of kids.

I couldn't help wondering what Daddy had for me. I just knew it was a pocketknife. There was a box of scrap wood pieces out on the back porch, and I'd taken to carving names in them; I'd done one for Daddy, Isabella and Mama. I would have done one for me and Jesse, but Mama and Isabella said that the steak knives and butcher knife I'd been using were too dangerous. Daddy thought so, too, but he stuck his block that said "Fred" up on a shelf in the store. A pocketknife wouldn't be dangerous, and there were always two or three in the pawn box.

But when I got to the store I checked the box and didn't see anything but two clock radios. I had a radio, and I didn't have any trouble getting up in the morning.

"It's not in there," Daddy said. "Wouldn't fit." He unlocked the warehouse door, and I followed him in.

"Go down around the corner and let me know what you think."

I ran. It was a piano. A big, shiny black piano. I touched one of the keys; it made a soft sound. Daddy put his hand on my shoulder. "Sit down and play a tune."

"I don't know how to play a piano, Daddy."

"Well, we're going to get you lessons, if that's what you want."

"Yes sir." I couldn't get over it. "Where'd it come from?"

"You know Johnny Chastain?"

My hands went up, and I stepped away. Johnny Chastain, playing loud with all his windows open, could just cover you up with music on a hot afternoon. Nobody on the Hard Road minded, except maybe his wife, Vella, who always said, if you mentioned it, "Don't be talking to me about no piano playing now." One night Cecil B. did a show at the store, and Johnny Chastain pushed his piano — this very piano! — out into the road and played. I went into my room and heard him playing right there on the radio.

"He came up one day with this thing in the back of a truck wanting to pawn it for thirty dollars, and I told him, I said, 'Johnny, you're crazy. I might deal with a watch or a clock radio now and again, but I'm not facilitated to deal with something like this,' " Daddy said.

"Won't he come back for it?"

"Johnny Chastain's long gone." Daddy took my

hand. "Let's go talk to your mama about those piano lessons."

"I'm not so sure we should move Johnny's piano just yet," Mama said.

"He swore to me up and down that he'd come back for it. He promised me he wouldn't leave me with that thing taking up room — room I don't have."

"Well, what about Vella? No matter what the deal was between you and Johnny, it might be nice to just give it back to her."

"You don't think I thought about that?" Daddy was mad. "What do you think I am, her and that little girl left high and dry — "

"I heard Johnny just went up north for work."

"Well, all I know," Daddy said, "is that I offered to move it back to Vella's place, and she said if she never saw it again, it would be too soon."

"Well, just the same — "

"Why would I want to try to keep that boy's piano? He had to beg me to take it in the first place."

"I know, but — "

"I gave her something for it. I made it right. She said she hoped Rachel would enjoy it and to tell her she said so."

Mama smiled. "Okay, honey." She looked at me. "I think your grandma knows somebody that would come to the house for lessons. That sound good?"

I nodded.

* * *

49

The next day was the funeral service, so I didn't have to go to school. Daddy didn't think it was necessary for me to go to the funeral either, but Mama did. It was the sort of thing I could have gotten out of with just a little crying, but I knew Mama was right. It seemed like going could get me comfortable with my feelings.

Somebody in the church was wearing Old Spice, smelling just like Great-uncle Hewitt. There was a giant bowl of orange and white flowers, off to the side of me, smelling just like Grandma's flower garden at the old homeplace. Instead of the preacher talking over the coffin, I saw Great-uncle Hewitt, tall, without his cane, with his arm around Uncle Carter. They were both laughing. Grandma was there, and she wasn't grumpy. I couldn't remember the joke or when it was it happened, but I remembered the smells.

Before we'd left for the funeral, Daddy said that it sure wasn't necessary for me to view the body and all that. I could have just got up and walked in line with everybody else, but Daddy was right on that one. It wasn't necessary. In my mind I'd already seen Great-uncle Hewitt one last time.

That night I was waked up by screaming and yelling. I got up and looked through the blinds and saw the blond girl leaving in the pickup. The boy ran fast and jumped onto the tailgate. The next afternoon the FOR RENT sign was stuck back into the dirt yard.

"They didn't live there very long."

"No," Isabella said.

"Didn't you think it was funny, the way the boy was always working on that lawnmower, when they didn't even have any grass?"

"Funny?" Isabella shook her head. "No, I didn't think it was funny."

Seven

Cynthia asked me if I could come to her house after school. It was too cold to walk, so her mother picked us up. Mama would come by and pick me up at five-thirty before she went to take Isabella home.

Callie Thompson's mother was waiting for her, just like she was most every day, with the car door already open. Callie waved to us as she ran by.

"My mama doesn't believe it," Cynthia said, "but I told her that Callie Thompson's the smartest girl in our class."

"She sure knows something to say about everything."

Caroline's mother pulled up. "Isn't Caroline riding with us?" I asked. Caroline and Cynthia's mothers took turns picking them up when it was cold.

Cynthia shook her head. "She has ballet today."

Caroline pressed her face against the car window and stuck out her tongue.

I waved.

Cynthia shook her head.

I had expected that going home after school meant playing with Caroline, too. Caroline was fun, but it was kind of relaxing, just sitting at Cynthia's kitchen table. She cut two pieces of bread into eight triangles, spread them with butter, put triangles of American cheese on them, then toasted them. While we were eating them, Cynthia pointed out the window, down the street, toward a two-story yellow house. "She broke into that house."

I looked. "Who?"

"Caroline."

I couldn't believe it. "Were the people home?"

Cynthia shook her head. "Nobody lived there then, but while she was in there, the real estate lady came with some people, and all the kids were outside watching. The people went in, and we knew Caroline was still in there — "

"Did she get caught?"

Cynthia shook her head. "No," she said, "but she came this close" — her thumb and finger were touching — "to being caught."

"What happened?"

"She hid in a closet, listening to every word they said, until they left." Cynthia took a bite of her last cheese triangle. "My mama says Caroline just doesn't think."

"You told your mama?"

"Not about that." Cynthia stood up. "She just doesn't think about anything."

One whole side of Cynthia's room was Barbie Land, a tower of blue-and-pink-fabric-covered boxes that made up Barbie's apartment, the bank where she worked and the restaurant where Ken took her on dates. Cynthia had seven Barbies and two Kens of her own, and I'd thought about bringing my own Barbies over here, to give them a better home.

"That Barbie, the one with the black hair, her name is Sally," Cynthia said. Sally sat in the Barbie restaurant wearing a pink dress. "Put on the gold lamé, and then they can double-date."

I was glad when Cynthia was ready to do something else. Even in Barbie Land, I had a hard time getting anything going with Barbie. She pulled her knitting machine out of the closet. "Let's go out on the porch," she said.

I made red squares, and Cynthia stitched them together. "You can make a blanket, or a rug or even a purse."

I loved it. "Make a purse," I said. "I'll do red ones for one side, and blue ones for the other."

"Look! Look!"

Cynthia and I looked. Caroline was back from her ballet lesson. She ran across her driveway and held up her new sunglasses; one of the lenses was missing. "Oh," Cynthia said.

"I dropped them on the sidewalk, and it just fell out and cracked!" Caroline was happy about it.

"That's too bad," Cynthia said. She rolled her eyes at me.

"No, no, it's great. My mama's got this new shade of nail polish, kind of a pearly pink. Did I show you?"

Cynthia shook her head.

"Well, I'm going to poke out the other lens and then paint the empty frames that color, with the nail polish, and wear them like real glasses. Isn't that neat?" She ran back into her house to do it.

"She's crazy," Cynthia said.

They were neat. The next day Caroline wore hers to school. The day after that Cynthia and I had a pair. Mine were red because that was the only color Mama had. Cynthia's were the same pearly pink as Caroline's. By Wednesday Cynthia's mother had taken hers away because they were ridiculous, and Caroline had dropped hers again and cracked the frame, so she just threw them away. I loved mine.

I was careful with them at school, wearing them only at lunch, recess, at the reading table and while waiting for Mama to pick me up after school, never when Miss Evers was talking. She was always taking away "distractions" and putting them in her drawer.

"Miss Taylor said that if you didn't stop wearing those things you'd end up wearing glasses for real," Cynthia said.

"How do you know that?" Miss Taylor wasn't even a teacher. She was the principal's secretary.

"She told Caroline."

"So?" That Caroline carried on conversations with everybody.

"She said you sure wouldn't like it if you had to wear glasses for real."

I didn't mind a little attention. I just didn't want so much that I was a distraction.

I wore them at home in the afternoon while I did my homework or read. Isabella asked me about them once. "They're not real," I said and stuck my finger through to my eye. After that she just smiled and turned away. I didn't mind smiling, especially not the sweet way Isabella did it, but I took them off if I thought Aunt Celeste might drop by. She would probably like them — Aunt Celeste liked flashy things — but first she would laugh and tease me. I didn't want to be laughed at. And I never took the chance that Grandma Graham might see me in them.

I didn't hide them from Daddy, but it took him days to notice. I heard Mama and Daddy talking about them at night. "Do you think I should make her stop wearing them?" Mama said.

Daddy said, "I think they'll go away on their own."

"Don't forget," Miss Evers said, "the oral history report is due next Wednesday."

I hadn't forgotten, but I still didn't have any ideas. Last week Miss Evers took us to the school library, but every time anyone wandered past the biography section, she said, "Now, children, don't waste your time." She moved her hand up and down and cut us off. "This is where you'll find what you need." I liked to look. I couldn't concentrate, watching her arm like that, so I didn't find anything.

Mama promised to take me to the library downtown, and I wasn't surprised when I had to remind her, but I was real upset when then she said she couldn't go. "Your daddy's got a big order to put up," she said. "I've got to stay up front."

"We could go," Isabella said. "On the bus."

Mama went quiet. She was considering that same old bus story, worrying about what could happen to you getting on or off.

"I need to get started on it today," I said.

Mama brightened. "I could pick you all up, take you home from there."

"Yes ma'am," Isabella said.

"You don't mind?"

"No ma'am," Isabella said. She looked at me. "I think it might be fun."

I couldn't wait for Miss Perone to see my glasses. She'd only been the librarian since the middle of the summer, but already she called me by my name as soon as I walked in. She wore glasses that were shiny, a sort of white color, and had long hair pulled up high in a ponytail. Miss Perone was pretty.

The bus ride wasn't much. We had a little trouble getting Jesse's carriage inside, but the bus driver promised it would fit. "Company has to take babies and what have you into consideration," he said. He was right. His name was Howard, he told us, and it said so on his shirt. It was easier getting off because we'd figured out where the carriage caught the first time.

Jesse slept on the bus, and he didn't wake up until we were inside the library. Isabella picked him up and bounced him a bit. The public library was in the basement of the courthouse, so it was sort of dark to be a reading place. The only windows were narrow and on the same level as the street; you looked through them and all you saw of the outside was people's feet moving by.

"Hello, Rachel." Miss Perone spoke up, just like always. Her voice was deep, one that I'd like to have.

"Hello," I said.

"Jesse and I'll take a little walk," Isabella said. "You meet us out front."

"Don't you want to look around?"

"Well, maybe."

"Can Isabella check out a book on my card?" I asked.

Miss Perone nodded. "Well, surely, she can, but it's easy enough for Isabella to get her own card."

I liked it the way Miss Perone did that, said people's

58

names. My teacher this year, Miss Evers, she never said names, made you feel as if she forgot you from day to day.

Isabella got interested all of a sudden. She left the carriage and carried Jesse in her arms down to Miss Perone's desk. "Do I need to fill something out?"

Miss Perone pulled out a form. "All I need to see is something with your address on it."

Isabella shook her head.

"A checkbook?"

"No."

"Gas bill? Electric?"

"No ma'am. I live with my brother, and he — "

"Anything. A personal letter?"

Isabella smiled. I took Jesse from her — he didn't much like it — and she dug in her purse and pulled out a worn, white envelope.

Miss Perone looked it over. "This is fine." Isabella filled out her name and address, and Miss Perone typed it out on the card. "There you go," she said.

"Well," Isabella said to me, "I'm going to go find me a book." She looked back up at Miss Perone. "What time do you close, Miss?"

"Six."

"I'll take Jesse out if he gets restless," she said to me. "You take your time."

The library was crowded, stacked all the way to the ceiling, just like our rooms behind the store used to be, only they were never this dusty. I liked just walking and looking, pulling out books here and there. Something always turned up for me that way. At school they never turned us loose with the books without directions.

I had a general idea where to find the biographies. I'd checked out a real interesting one on Mozart this summer, but he wouldn't do. The report had to be on American history. I read the edge of a blue book. Eleanor Roosevelt. That was an idea.

"You working on your history report?"

I turned around. There stood Callie Thompson all done up in her Scout uniform. Caroline and Cynthia were Scouts, too, but I'd never been involved in too much after-school stuff.

"What's yours on?"

"I don't know," I said.

Callie Thompson was always straight and perfect, but she went even straighter at that. "How can you be working on it if you don't know what it's on?"

"I'm just looking."

"Mine's on the signing of the Constitution."

"Okay."

"They're due on Wednesday, you know."

"I know." I pulled out the Eleanor Roosevelt book and held on to it, just to show I knew what I was doing.

"I'll show you how to use the card catalogue."

"I know how. I know all about Dewey decimals." They went over and over it in school, every year, so you'd have to be a moron not to. "I'll find something."

Callie Thompson shook her three shiny ponytails. "Wasting your time," she said, but she let it go and went on about her business.

I held on to Eleanor Roosevelt and moved over to pull out a book with a yellow cellophane book jacket. It was on Thomas Paine. I read the back. He had something to do with America. I went around and grabbed a book on planets and another one on drawing people. It was ten before six. Callie Thompson was the one who had wasted my time.

"I like those glasses, Rachel," Miss Perone said. "They make you look French."

"I wish I was French," I said.

Miss Perone laughed, but it was a happy laugh, not a teasing one. "Me, too, Rachel," she said. "Me, too."

Isabella was sitting out front with Jesse and two books on her lap. The carriage was folded, so we could fit it into the trunk. "Did you find what you needed?"

I nodded. I showed her the two biographies. "Which one do you think I should use for school?"

"I don't know," she said. "Mrs. Roosevelt was a fine, fine woman, but I don't know much about Mr. Paine."

I didn't think to wonder about Isabella's books until Mama had already let her out of the car and left her at her house.

* * *

61

On Saturday Daddy was able to get this fellow Al to help him load the piano into the pickup and put it in the house. The chair and the table next to the French doors in the living room were moved next to the window to make space. Even though the piano was little as far as pianos go — it wasn't one of those big, open affairs like you saw on television — Daddy and Al stopped on every step to take a breath.

I was out front watching when suddenly the yard was swarming like somebody had stepped on an anthill. All these kids were running around me, yelling, not saying anything to me, just yelling. They were spinning around so fast I couldn't get fixed on how many there were altogether.

They surprised Daddy when he came out the front door. Al just laughed and waved at them like flies. "Get on out of the way," Daddy said. "I got to pull this truck out now." He looked at me like I knew what was going on.

Just as quickly as they popped up, they scattered and disappeared, all except for the big one. She was older than me, with black, fringy hair, a red dress and a long purple nylon scarf around her neck. She just stood there, like a statue, until Daddy turned the corner off of Brown Street.

"Hello," Isabella said from the front porch.

"I can play that thing," the girl said.

Isabella opened the door. "Well, come on in and play something for us."

I didn't know how Mama would feel about strangers in the house, but it was done now, so I followed the girl inside. She sat down on the bench. "This one's called 'Heart and Soul,' " she said. "Do you know that one?"

Isabella and I shook our heads. The girl smiled and bounced her head along with her fingers. She could play.

"That's very good," Isabella said.

"Here's another one." This one was faster.

"I think I heard that one before," Isabella said.

"That one's called 'Chopsticks,' and it's easier than that other one." She looked at me. "You want to learn it?"

Isabella gave me a push. Who was this person? I sat down beside her. "Just watch," she said. She played the song again and said, "Okay, you try." It was easy. After three tries and watching her one more time, I got it perfect.

"You know any hymns?" Isabella asked.

"No ma'am. I wish." She twirled the scarf into a knot. "I don't have any place to practice or anything." She stood up. "I have to go."

"Well, this here's Rachel, and I'm Isabella."

"I'm Pamela Tucker, ma'am."

"Well, thank you very much for the music."

And Pamela Tucker opened the front screen door herself and walked out. You'd think she'd be the one to say thank you. Isabella looked out the door and saw her running into the dirt yard of the white house.

When Mama came to take Isabella home, I was still playing "Chopsticks." "Well, I never. You learned a song already?"

Isabella got her purse. She didn't say a word about Pamela Tucker. Neither did I.

Eight

None of those Tucker kids were in my grade at school, and that was fine with me. You could hear them out front in the morning, waiting for the school bus, yelling like a bunch of animals. They didn't bother me much directly because I kept a watch through my bedroom window; if they were out, I'd stay in, or either I'd slip through the back door and stay in the far corner of the yard, next to Miss Peaks's, so that they couldn't see me. Usually they were outside, crawling all over the rusted-out station wagon and flatbed truck parked in their yard.

One afternoon, though, they sneaked up on me, yelling and climbing the fence. I raced into the kitchen. "Isabella! Those kids are getting in our yard."

Isabella should have seen the whole thing through the window. She was pushing Jesse back and forth in his carriage, with her foot, and clucking at him. He was fussy, but she couldn't pick him up because she had flour on her hands. "What are their names?"

"I don't know."

"How old are they?"

"I don't know."

"You should know. They're your neighbors."

"They're climbing right over! Look at that one, pulling on Miss Peaks's tree."

"Well, you go out there and tell him he shouldn't do that, that he should use the gate."

I looked at her like she was crazy. "You think they're going to listen to me?"

"If they don't, I'll come tell them, but I want to see you try first."

"You want me to go out there?"

"Yes ma'am. And when you come back in, I want you to tell me the names of each and every one of them — and a little something special about each one."

I looked at her hard, but I went out. I did what I had to do, then came back in with my report. I tried to keep my voice as flat and ugly as their dirty faces. "Sue, she should be in my grade, but she's only in third. She doesn't talk much. Then there's Terry. He's goofy. He's in third, too, even though they say Sue's older. I don't know why it is they're in the same grade. They don't either. Curt's five. He's sneaky mean. Boyd's just two, way too little to be running around in somebody else's yard."

"So there's five Tucker children altogether."

"Yes ma'am, but that Pamela, she wasn't with them. She was just sitting on their truck, watching."

Isabella nodded. "That's nice."

"I don't see why you force me to talk to them. They don't have any manners at all."

"Well, no matter what we think, people have faces and names and come from particular places. And we don't always choose our neighbors."

I guess it made Isabella happy that I knew their names, but I kept up my trick of checking out the window and hiding on the far side of the yard. I looked directly at Pamela Tucker, even when we just drove by. She sat and stared, and she scared me.

Miss Love, the piano teacher, was shorter than Miss Peaks, and if you looked only at her feet, wrapped in strapped, black flats, arched, with toes pointed to touch the floor, you would think she was a little kid. But above her feet she was all grown up. She wore straight skirts and jackets to match. Her hair was pulled into a tight ball at the back of her head. She sat in the rocking chair while I sat at the piano following her instructions.

"Slow . . . down. Feel the Beat." Miss Love's head and hands moved with her words. They tried to move with my music. Her eyes were closed.

I chanted the lyrics in my head. "Here we go, up a row." I played with one finger.

Somehow Miss Love knew. "Fingering," she said. I shifted back into position.

"Turn the page," she said. I did. "Before next week, I want you to do the timing exercises."

"Do I go on to the next song?"

"No, continue with today's songs." She stood up and leaned over me. "When I give an assignment, always pencil in the date on the top of the page." She did it for me.

The three dollars for the lesson lay beside the music. I picked it up and gave it to her.

"Thank you, my dear." She unsnapped her small black purse and tucked the money inside. She rested her hand on my head, just for a moment, and said, "Practice. Practice."

"Yes ma'am," I said.

Miss Love looked, with her hair and sharp nose, like a music teacher who would rap knuckles, but she didn't. Miss Love was almost as fair and understanding as Isabella. Sometimes she would even say, "Very good, Rachel," but I was never very good. Sometimes I wished she wasn't so nice, that she would rap me, that she would make me practice, make me play good music.

After my second lesson with Miss Love, when she went outside to her round, old-fashioned gray car, Pamela Tucker was sitting on our front steps. "Hey," she said to Miss Love, not to me.

"Hello, young lady," Miss Love said. She drove

away, and I just went back inside. I peeped out after a minute, and Pamela Tucker was gone.

The next Tuesday, though, when Miss Love left, and she was there again, I said, "Come on in."

Pamela Tucker didn't say thanks or anything else. She sat right down, hunched over the keyboard. She worked out the "Here We Go" song, then moved on to the next one and then the next one.

"I'm not on that one yet," I said.

"I am," she said.

After a while, I tapped her on the shoulder, hurrying her along. "My mama doesn't like me having people in the house, not when I still have homework."

"Just give me a minute," she said.

"Don't be telling Sue and the rest of them about this. You can't all be coming in here. My mama would have a fit."

"You think I want those brats running around me any more than they already do?" She got that third song perfect, then stood up to leave. "Bye," she said.

Every Tuesday after that was the same. I always got her out before six o'clock without any trouble; I don't think she particularly wanted to see if Mama really would have a fit or not. Sometimes I said, "Very good, Pamela." I didn't say it sweetly like Miss Love. I said it mean and sarcastic, but just the same it was, and I meant it.

I didn't practice much at first, except for Tuesday, right before Miss Love showed up, but when we took up playing with two hands at the same time, I figured I had to. Isabella said she wouldn't force me to practice, but she prayed that I would see the value of doing a thing well and that I would respect the fact that my mama and daddy worked hard to give me privileges. I felt forced, but more by Pamela Tucker than Isabella or even Miss Love. Pamela Tucker walked in the Tuesday before, turned the page and said, "Oh, this one's hands together," and just did it.

"Why do you think Miss Love says, 'Very good, Rachel'?" I asked Isabella. "She knows it's not true."

"Maybe she's just encouraging you because she knows you're doing the best you can do."

"I could do better." That was a horrible thought, that Miss Love might not think so. "It just all seems so easy for Pamela Tucker."

Isabella smiled. "Well now, you have to remember she's older — "

"So?"

"Well, that can make things easier. Some things that are very hard just come together with a little aging."

"So I'll be better when I'm twelve?"

"If you want to, if you practice."

"Pamela Tucker doesn't have anyplace to practice."

"Well, that might just be her secret."

"What?"

"Being without, that can give a body such a pure wanting to."

70

"So it's sort of a miracle that she can play like that."
Isabella shook her head. "A gift."

One of the books Miss Love had given me was a hymnal, and even though she didn't think I was ready for hymns yet, Pamela Tucker was trying to pick some out already. "It probably bothers you when I practice, though, it sounds so bad."

Isabella finished folding the last of the towels. That was one way Isabella and Mama were alike; you either had to catch them doing a standing-still job if you wanted to talk or you had to follow them around. "I like to hear you play, as long as you're working sweet and patient, not banging and mad." She took a stack of towels, and I took one, too, and followed her into the bathroom.

"Who plays piano at your church?"

"We don't have one."

"You don't have music?" I thought of that as the main part of church, the singing.

"Oh, we sing, Rachel. We sing loud. We just don't have a piano."

We went back for more clothes. Isabella took Daddy's undershirts, and I took Jesse's diapers. He was awake and stretching in his crib, so I picked him up and brought him out. Isabella slowed down for Jesse. "Your brother's the preacher, isn't he? Can't he get a piano for the church?"

"Well, the truth is, my brother Gary is what you call a deacon, but that does make him the leader of our congregation. And you might say we don't really have a church — we just all get together in the front room of our house."

"Oh." Jesse stretched and made noises like he might cry.

"I think he needs a change." She took him from me and kissed him on the head.

"I'll get him some juice," I said.

Isabella was sitting in the living room and waiting for the juice. She patted the seat beside her on the couch. "It's not a bad thing, Rachel, having our church right there in our home. When I went up and joined my brother and his new church, when I cast aside my old complications and took on the path of the Mennonites, it was the most wonderful day of my life."

Sometimes I felt like that in church, after a really good Sunday school story, or a lot of singing, but I couldn't carry that feeling all the time. If we managed to get to church all the time, like Isabella, maybe I could. But then it was probably easier if the church was right there in your house.

Isabella laughed. "I went up to meet Gary, not knowing whether he'd really found the way or whether he was just in some sort of a jam — he could be wild as a boy — but it was the real thing all right. Some of the elders were talking to me about their beliefs and ways, and one of them said that I shouldn't cut my hair anymore. And I piped right up and said, 'Oh, I've never cut my hair, sir,' and they looked at me like 'Girl, how can you be lying to us now?' There wasn't a hair on my head more than an inch long."

"You lied?" I couldn't believe it, and if Isabella did lie, I didn't want to know about it.

"No." She flipped Jesse over on her lap to burp him. "All of a sudden I realized what they were seeing, what they were thinking, and I said, 'Oh, I didn't cut it, it was burned off.' You should have seen their faces. So I explained to them about being young and foolish and overusing the hot comb."

"What?"

Isabella put Jesse up on her shoulder. "A hot comb's just that, a heated comb that silly black girls like me use to straighten their hair."

"Why?"

Isabella shook her head. "It never will grow back, not like it was."

I could see she was getting ready to put Jesse down, that she was about to get busy again. "Isabella, why doesn't your brother Gary like us?"

Isabella opened her mouth. "Why, Rachel, Gary knows you're all fine people. He even told me, after you called me up that time, that he thinks you're a real polite little girl."

I shook my head. "He looks mad when we bring you home. He turns real quick, so he won't have to see us, and he won't ever wave."

Isabella looked down. She tapped her finger on my

knee. She looked back up. "It doesn't have anything to do with you and your family. He doesn't mean to act that way. It's just that he doesn't like the idea that I clean somebody else's house, that that's what I do for my job."

I didn't say anything. That's what she did. She cleaned our house up and down every day. She ironed our clothes and cooked our meals, but that's not all she did.

"It doesn't have anything to do with you at all."

"Is it not a good job?"

Isabella pressed Jesse closer with one hand and took my hand with her other one. "It's a wonderful job. I love you and Jesse with all my heart."

"Can't you tell him that?"

"That's the part he doesn't like the most, when I say you're like my family. He says I can be let go. He says real family can't be let go." She stood up. "I've got to get busy."

I stood up, too. "I'm going to learn a hymn for you. Which is your favorite one?"

"Any one you would play for me, Rachel, that would be my favorite."

I went over and over that hands-together song. I was getting it. My hands were working together instead of one always following the other one. My eyes filled up with tears, and some of them ran down my face. I was crying, but it was the kind of crying you could stand back and think about because why you were crying wasn't clear, so the tears were a surprise. I pulled my hands off the keyboard. Nothing was for sure. This piano wasn't mine. It belonged to Johnny Chastain. It even belonged to Pamela Tucker, even though she had no right, just because of that pure wanting to.

Nine

We weren't going over to Grandma Graham's on Saturday afternoon to eat. We were just supposed to drop off a box of groceries and say hello. "Stay for supper," Grandma said. She had turnip greens, potatoes and field peas going on the stove, and I knew she was bound to make a pan of cornbread.

"I got some things to tend to at home, Mama," Mama said.

"Well, now that's just fine, but what are you feeding this child?"

"Soup and sandwich."

"Well, isn't that just fine. I've got all this good food, Carter's too busy out catting around and you want to feed this child a cold sandwich."

"We'll stay."

"I say what's the point in having children if you get too busy to care for them."

"We'll stay."

It was a good supper. I'd learned to like greens as long as there was vinegar, onions and cornbread to go with them. Jesse fussed a little, wiggling around in Mama's lap, but Uncle Carter showed up after all, so I thought it might all be fine.

"Where's that girl tonight?" Grandma asked.

"Working," Uncle Carter said.

"Guess you're going to have to get married soon."

"I don't know, Mama." Uncle Carter reached out for the peas. Mama gave him the bowl.

"Well, I know. I guess you're going to want to move all the old stuff out of here, make room for your wife's new things."

"Mama — " Mama said.

"And I would imagine that would include me."

"Mama," Uncle Carter said. He finished his chewing before he said, "You and all your things are here for as long as you want them to be."

"Oh, that's just lovely. You're just going to sit around and wait for me to die every day for the rest of my natural life."

Jesse let out an awful scream. "I better get this one home and to bed," Mama said. I could have hugged and kissed Jesse for that scream.

"I thought Grandma liked Miss Macy now," I said to Mama in the car.

"I don't know," she mumbled. She didn't want to talk about it to me, but she sure talked about it that

77

night when Daddy got home from work. "Carter just sits there, takes it, says, 'Yes ma'am,' 'No, ma'am.' I'd go right through the roof."

"Well now, Bobbie," Daddy said, "he lives with her. He's got to keep the peace."

I lay in bed, listening, knowing that Daddy was exactly right, thinking back to some of those whole days I'd spent with Grandma before Isabella came. I'd watch what I said, tiptoe and sneak around. I figured I had to do that, being a kid and all, but the idea of a grown man doing that didn't seem right.

On Sunday afternoon Uncle Carter came by to visit, and he brought Macy Mitchell with him. She had on a big flowery dress, and she wanted to hug everybody. Uncle Carter looked small beside her, but he looked happy. Mama set out bowls of banana pudding and glasses of iced tea in the living room.

"Do you like your Uncle Carter's new tie?" she said to me.

"Yes ma'am," I said. "I guess I do." I couldn't remember if I'd ever seen Uncle Carter wear a tie, not even when he was on his way to church.

I still thought Macy's hair was beautiful. I wanted to touch it, but she was a hugger, so I hung back for the time being.

"We don't want to take up your whole afternoon," Uncle Carter said. "We just wanted to drop by because, well, you need to get to know Macy better because — "

Uncle Carter stopped talking. I looked up. There was Aunt Celeste, opening up the front door, and Grandma Graham was following right behind her.

"Well, hey, gang," Aunt Celeste said. The way she turned her head toward Mama and widened her eyes, I could tell she didn't expect to see the others there.

"Carter," Grandma said, "what a surprise." She didn't seem surprised. She nodded her head at Macy.

Aunt Celeste helped Mama bring in more banana pudding and iced tea. I tried to follow them into the kitchen, but Mama said, "You stay put."

"Now how'd you do this custard?" Grandma Graham said.

"The usual way," Mama said.

"It's delicious," Uncle Carter said.

"Mmmm," Macy said. Her mouth was full.

"What'd you use?" Grandma said. "Cornstarch?"

"No ma'am," Mama said. "Flour."

Grandma nodded. "Measure it out exactly, did you?"

"How much should I have used?"

"I don't measure myself," Grandma Graham said, "but I find most people have to be more careful with custard."

Uncle Carter set his empty bowl on the coffee table. I slipped out of the room and looked in on Jesse. Still sleeping. I thought about waking him up, just to take him in there and create a newer, nicer commotion.

Babies were good for that. I thought about it and listened.

"Did we interfere with something?" Grandma Graham said. "I guess we should have called."

"Just a little visit," Uncle Carter said.

"We were passing by," Macy said.

"Not planning any surprises?" Grandma Graham said. "Not setting a date?"

"Date?" Uncle Carter said.

"You been married before?" Grandma Graham said.

I moved to the door and watched. Uncle Carter, Aunt Celeste and even Mama were looking down at their laps. Macy and Grandma Graham stared at each other like arm wrestlers. "Yes ma'am, I have," Macy said.

"I heard all about it at the nursing home, you know, when I was there visiting Hewitt."

I moved back to Jesse's crib and picked him up, bouncing him to wake him up.

"You must remember, Miss Graham," Macy said, "many of those people you spoke with at the nursing home are not completely in their right mind."

I rushed into the room. Jesse came to wildly, looking around. "Look who's here!" I said.

"Ooooh," Macy said, "let me have that baby."

Aunt Celeste gave me such a smile. I'd never felt so much a part of the family.

* * *

Jesse didn't crawl proper, not up on his hands and knees like he was supposed to, but he scooted flat on his belly, twisting his elbows back and forth to get him going. It was sort of like those soldiers you see in the movies, sliding in the mud to keep out of the gunfire. Isabella was ironing, but she said he could stay on the floor as long as I watched him and kept him away from the ironing board. I got on the floor with him and followed him around.

"Did you have a good weekend?" Isabella asked.

My head filled up with Macy and Uncle Carter and Grandma Graham. "Are you going to get married, Isabella?"

"Child," Isabella said, "what put that question in your head?"

"Do you have a boyfriend?"

Isabella shook her head. "No, I do not."

"You're pretty," I said. "You ought to have one."

"Pretty don't have nothing to do with it," Isabella said. "The young black men I've known, well, they didn't seem to have much interest in the straight and narrow."

"What about your brother?"

She stopped her ironing and looked at me. "Well, for goodness sakes, Rachel, he's my brother, and he's married to boot."

"Do you wish they did?"

"What?"

"Wish the young black men had — "

"Rachel, Rachel, don't be worrying about me or the young black men. A little age might straighten them out." Her voice went serious. "I think you might be listening to those radio songs a little too much." Isabella did not like rock and roll. She never said so directly. I just knew.

"I think maybe my Uncle Carter's getting married."

"Oh." She put her foot out to stop Jesse.

I scooted him back out of the way. "I think that's fine, but I sure hope my Aunt Celeste doesn't get married."

"Well now, Rachel," Isabella said, "from what I hear your Aunt Celeste doesn't feel exactly the same way."

I lay down and let Jesse scoot against me. "I guess."

"Why wouldn't you want her to get married?"

"I don't know."

Aunt Celeste lived in an apartment and wasn't scared to ride the bus back and forth to her job at the flower shop every day. Once or twice I'd spent the afternoon with her at work, watching her fix up arrangements, making good-luck horseshoes out of gladiolas and casket blankets out of carnations.

Grandma Graham made up flower arrangements, too. She was always putting together something from her garden for Sunday services or somebody's wedding or party. She fixed up flowers for our dining table just about every week. "Your Grandma's got a wicked tongue on occasion," Mama said, "but to grow roses like she does, she's got to have a good heart."

I asked Aunt Celeste once, when I was at her shop, if she took up flower arranging from Grandma.

"I didn't take anything from her," Aunt Celeste said. "I took up flower arranging because I had to do something." Aunt Celeste was always madder at Grandma than Mama ever was.

"It's not right," Grandma Graham said time and again, "for a woman to live alone like that. She ought to settle down. She ought to marry."

Aunt Celeste's apartment wasn't very nice. Even Mama said that. It was in a low brick building, with only one window and a row of round metal clotheslines out back. The one thing Aunt Celeste did have was lots of fancy shoes; the last time I was over there I tried on two pairs of red high heels, five pairs of sandals, a pair of blue and yellow flats with bows and a pair of clear plastic pumps with rhinestone heels. I just couldn't see a person being married and still having those kinds of shoes.

Ten

There had always been extra things to do after school, but when I first started to school Mama and Daddy were working so hard that there just wasn't time for me to get involved in anything like Scouts or chorus. Getting me to and from school was complicated enough without worrying about something meeting on Wednesday afternoons or Saturday mornings. I guess it got less complicated as I got older, but I just never got into the habit of getting involved in those things. Cynthia and Caroline were Scouts. I never thought about it.

Maybe I thought about it a little on Thursdays, when most of the other girls came dressed in their green Scout dresses, but I didn't think about it enough in between to do anything about it. It was Missy Harris's mom that dragged me into the Scouts.

Miss Harris didn't do her main shopping at our store, but she was always stopping by for milk or bread or potato chips. She was one of the Scout leaders, and she asked Mama why didn't I come to the meetings.

"I don't know," Mama said. "Thursdays can be busy around here."

"If a ride's the only thing holding her back, send her on to the meeting Thursday, and I'll drop her here when it's over." Miss Harris paid for her milk and said, "Nine times out of ten I'm stopping by here anyway. We're always needing something."

So I got suited up and the next Thursday I was a Scout. It really wasn't much, just a noisy bunch of girls with dimes. The leaders, Miss Harris and Miss Ambersmith, outlined upcoming projects, took up dimes and tried to calm the girls down. It was more school, only wilder.

All the other Scouts had at least one badge sewn onto their sashes, mostly the one with little crossed spoons and a bowl. According to my handbook that was the one for cooking. Callie Thompson had that one and three others. I tried to see what the other three were for.

"What are you looking at?" Callie snapped.

"Your badges," I said. "What's that one? Sewing?"

"Yes," she said. She pointed to the next one. "And this one's for first aid." Her finger moved down to the crossed paintbrushes. "And this one's art."

"You're the only one with four," I said.

"I know," Callie said.

The only business that really got taken care of was that next meeting we would celebrate International Day. We were all supposed to bring a present, that should cost no more than fifty cents, to put into the piñata. We were doing Mexico.

"Can it cost a quarter?" Caroline asked.

"It can cost nothing at all and still be a nice present," Miss Harris said.

"You might draw a nice picture," Miss Ambersmith said.

"But if you decide to purchase a present," said Miss Harris, "be sure to spend no more than fifty cents."

"I'm bringing a real fifty-cent gift," Caroline said. "So don't anybody bring me a homemade picture." The girls around her laughed.

Even though it had been her idea, I was afraid Miss Harris might forget all about me when it was time to go home. The best thing to do, I figured, would be to hang around Missy Harris, but she was so skinny and shy she shook all the time. She scared me.

"How do you like it?" Caroline said.

"What?"

"Scouts, dummy."

"Oh yeah. I like it," I said.

"You got to be a Scout," she said. "You going to camp?"

I looked around for Miss Harris. I didn't want to be left alone in the school cafeteria. She was still packing up her papers and books. "I don't know." I didn't know what she was talking about.

"Oh, you have to go to camp," Caroline said. "We'll be camp buddies."

"What?"

"That's like partners. You have to have one. Buddies do everything together."

"Yeah." I smiled. "That sounds great."

"Caroline!" Cynthia was motioning for her to come outside. Her mama was taking them both home.

"Bye," she said and ran to the door.

There wasn't much danger of Miss Harris forgetting me because she had to wait until everyone had been picked up before she could leave, and, of course, I was still there. I sat between Missy Harris and Miss Harris in the car. Miss Harris kept telling Missy to tell me things, like what Missy was getting for her birthday and how her science project was coming along, but Missy wasn't quick enough, so Miss Harris would jump right in and tell me about them herself. Missy Harris didn't say a word the entire trip to the store. "Well, believe it or not," Miss Harris said when she pulled up in front of the store, "I don't need any milk today. Tell Rachel bye-bye, Missy. Well, bye-bye, Rachel." Missy gave a weak little wave.

"Bye, Missy," I said. Mama was checking an order of candy. She said I could have some juice or chocolate milk, and then when she finished we'd go get Isabella and take her home. I took my chocolate milk out front and looked down the street beside the store. It wasn't just Jeannette and Tamara, there weren't any kids anymore, nothing but old people in old houses. Even Johnny Chastain's wife, Vella, had moved back to the country with her parents.

I thought the first badge I'd go for would be one that nobody else had, not even Callie Thompson. Music.

I told Pamela Tucker about it when she came over after Miss Love left on Tuesday. She didn't look at me. She just sat on the piano stool and flipped ahead in the book.

"I could play some little song, that's all," I said, "for the activity part. I think there's a piano in the auditorium."

Pamela Tucker laughed.

"Or I could sing something. It says that's okay."

Pamela Tucker snorted.

"What?"

She pushed hard away from the keyboard. I almost fell off the bench. "You and your fat-cheeked little baby and your nigger maid — "

"You better not — " I looked at the French doors. They were open.

Pamela Tucker looked, too. "I'm not saying anything bad about anybody. I'm trash and that's worse than being a" — her voice lowered to a whisper — "nigger. Don't you know? All I'm saying is just

88

because you got somebody paid to iron creases in your clothes and keep your nose clean and hair brushed don't make you any better than me."

"You better — "

"I mean, look at you. You wear the same stupid dress to school every day." She slammed the door on her way out.

"Pamela Tucker can't come back here anymore," I told Isabella.

"I don't think that's very kind," Isabella said.

I couldn't believe Isabella hadn't heard her. The doors were open. "She made fun of my clothes."

"She's jealous. She's not lucky enough to have nice things like you."

"She called you a nigger maid!" I gasped and stepped back when I said the word. I shouldn't have said it.

"Well," said Isabella quietly, "I guess that's what I am."

"You are not!" The tears exploded. I grabbed her around the waist. "Nigger" was ugly and mean. "Maid" was ice-cold. Those words had nothing to do with Isabella.

Isabella knelt down. "No, of course not. I'm sorry." She hugged me closer. Jesse was crawling on the floor, pushing right between us.

Isabella pulled back, held my shoulders and looked into my eyes. "We cannot be unkind. We must give all we have."

"She is right, you know, about my clothes."

"What do you mean?" Isabella said. "You have lovely clothes, and you know it."

"They're all the same dress. That thing of Mama's — the red and brown and green will make it a brand-new dress every day — that's the stupidest thing ever."

Isabella gave me a look. "Don't speak any disrespect about your mother. I won't stand for it."

Pamela Tucker got away with saying anything she wanted. I couldn't even complain about having to wear the same dress to school every single day.

The next Tuesday Miss Love came and left, and Pamela Tucker was waiting just like always. I let her in. She didn't say she was sorry, and I didn't ask her to. She opened the hymnal and figured out "On Calvary." Isabella came in and listened.

Eleven

As the school year went on, kids began to get out of alphabetical order because of not being able to see the board, being too short or too tall or just because of acting up. Caroline got moved away from Cynthia for acting up so that she was on the other side of me. She started talking to me all the time now, but she didn't play tricks on me. She only seemed to have an interest in doing that to Cynthia. "She's so prissy," Caroline said. "I think it's funny, the way she squeals."

One day when we were lining up for recess, Caroline said, "How come I don't come over to your house one day and play?"

It was the same thing, really, as Scouts. I knew why I never had people come over when we lived in the store; Mama'd convinced me that it would be too hard for other people to understand why we lived there. Plus it was too hard to work and keep up with other people's children at the same time. One of the things she'd said about the house was that I could have friends come over to visit. But just like getting involved in extra stuff after school, you had to get into the habit of inviting people over.

I shrugged. "Why don't you?"

"Well, when?"

Mama said that either after school on Wednesday or Saturday morning. Caroline picked Saturday.

I asked her if she wanted to play the piano, but she said no. She had brought her Barbies. We spread a blanket out under the pecan tree to play. Every time I played with Caroline we tried to get something going with the Barbies, but we never could seem to do it. We needed Cynthia for that. I think that was another reason I hadn't invited them over. It was hard to get them to agree on anything, like when and if to go somewhere, but on Chinaberry Lane we were usually together, the three of us.

"Is it haunted over there?" Caroline crawled toward the Haynes place and stared through the fence.

"I think so."

"What's that?" she said.

I looked. "Just a rock."

"Let's go see."

I shook my head.

"Why not? You scared?"

"No. It's not my property."

Caroline shrugged.

Through the Haynes trees I could see that Curt Tucker boy sticking his head out a window. When they moved in all the windows had screens. Not anymore. I knew Pamela Tucker wouldn't come anywhere near us, but I hoped the little ones wouldn't start whooping it up. I didn't want my neighbors acting trashy while I had company.

"What's that?" Caroline was on Miss Peaks's side now. Miss Peaks was on her knees, mixing in black dirt with her regular dirt. She looked up and said, "Those are my crocuses, dear, my messengers of an early spring."

There were so many of them bunched together, into a big purple circle, that I couldn't believe I hadn't noticed them before.

Miss Peaks stood up and smiled at us. She was short, white-haired and very brown. "Come around here and take a look. The only bad thing about crocuses is they're here today and gone tomorrow." Isabella had talked and waved to Miss Peaks, and she had given us jars of fig preserves and stuff, but our business had always been over the fence. She motioned Caroline and me over and unlatched her gate. "You girls come through there and have a seat on the bench. I'll go get us some iced tea."

We walked under a trellis holding up thick, twisting vines and sat down. You couldn't see all this through Miss Peaks's fruit trees. It was amazing. It smelled like the outdoors, but it felt like a cool room; the vines made a ceiling. Miss Peaks came back out with a tray and passed us our glasses. They all had little leaves in them.

"Is this parsley?" Caroline said.

"Mint, my dear," Miss Peaks said.

She held her glass high and moved it around. "Now this," she said, "is an English landscape garden. My husband, the late Mr. Peaks, designed it."

I knew I should introduce Caroline, but Miss Peaks didn't give me a chance.

"Do you know why I call this an English landscape garden?"

We shook our heads.

"Because you can't just say that, you know. There are special conditions that must be met." She sipped her tea, then set her glass down beside me on the bench. "There must be a bench," she said, "but not just any bench." She rubbed her fingers on the edge. "It must be a curved bench. Mr. Peaks carved the curves in this wood."

Caroline and I both felt the curves on our sides.

She pointed up. "There must be an arbor with parallel colonnades, a pergola, like you passed through."

We looked back and nodded.

"There must be water." She pointed to a small pond. Two orange fish flitted through it. A giant ceramic frog stood at one edge. "There must be a ruin."

94

She moved over to a pile of rocks. "It doesn't have to be a real ruin. It can be a facsimile, like this one here. See how Mr. Peaks built this up to look like an abandoned stone chimney?"

We nodded.

"And finally," Miss Peaks said, "there must be a grave."

Caroline gasped.

Miss Peaks laughed. "Specifically, a pet grave."

"Oh," Caroline said.

"Now, Mr. Peaks and me, we never bothered to have a pet, but — " She motioned for us to follow her back into a corner. There was a big stone with the word Conga carved in it. "My niece's cat was run over — by her husband, unfortunately, right in her own driveway — and she let us bury it here. And so, with that, we met all the conditions and could then officially call this our English landscape garden."

"Wow," Caroline said.

When we said good-bye, I said, "Miss Peaks, why do they call this Brown Street?"

She looked confused. "I don't know."

Isabella and Jesse were in the backyard rolling the ball. "You ever been back there?" Caroline said.

"No, I haven't," Isabella said.

"It's great."

Isabella smiled. "Miss Peaks is very good at growing things."

"They have a dead cat back there," Caroline said.

Isabella looked at me.

"It's for a special kind of garden, you've got to have one. Or a dog, or something."

"Oh," Isabella said.

"I like that hat," Caroline said.

Isabella smiled.

"It's not a hat," I said.

"Well, what is it then?"

"Isabella wears it for her religion, don't you, Isabella?"

"Yes."

"Are you a Baptist?"

Isabella shook her head. "I'm a Mennonite," she said.

"Wow." Caroline and I went around front to wait. Her mother was going to pick Caroline up on her way downtown to do some errands. "I like your house," she said.

So did I, more than I ever had before, but all the same I had to say, "It's not as nice as on Chinaberry Lane."

"It's better."

"Why?"

"Well, for one thing, we don't have a nigger maid. That's different."

Caroline's mother rounded the corner. I stared at her car, hoping it would move faster and take Caroline away. It was way worse when she said it than when

Pamela Tucker said it because she said it in a normal, nice voice, not in a mad way like Pamela Tucker. And it was way worse because I didn't say a thing about it, except "Bye" and then "Me, too" when she said she had had a good time. And I didn't mention anything about it to Isabella.

Twelve

I'd gotten out of the habit of wearing my red glasses except when Isabella took me to the library. Everyone else, I knew, was just waiting for me to get tired of them, but Miss Perone, I thought, really liked them.

"You still think you'd like to speak French?" Miss Perone said. Isabella had returned her book and was already pushing Jesse around on the other side, just like she always did.

I'd already picked out three books, a biography of Marie Curie, a book on rockets and a book on drawing flowers. "Yes ma'am, that's what I'm going to take when I can, in high school, I guess."

"No need to wait all that long," Miss Perone said. "Do you have a record player at home, Rachel?"

"Yes ma'am."

She held up her finger. "Wait right here just a minute," she said. Another girl stopped her, Miss Perone pointed out one of the stacks and then went into a back room.

A boy came in and returned a book to Miss Perone's desk. I picked it up. The Roman Empire sounded good.

"Here we are," Miss Perone said. She held up a record album with the Eiffel Tower on the front.

"Oh," I said, "I don't have a big record player, just a little one."

"Oh," Miss Perone said. "It only plays forty-fives?"

I nodded.

She looked around, then knelt down beside me. "I'm going to do something, but let's keep it a secret, okay?"

"Okay."

She motioned for me to follow her to the back room. It was a mess inside. She had to move boxes so I could sit on a stool. "Don't tell anyone because I just don't have the facility to do this for everyone." She moved some papers and opened up the record player on the desk. She put on the record album and said, "Don't try to understand. Just listen. Just have fun and sing along." She closed the door, then opened it again. "Sing quietly."

I stayed in there until Isabella came looking for me. I didn't know what it meant, but it sounded beautiful. Miss Perone told Isabella where I was right off, so I guess it wasn't supposed to be a secret from her. Miss Perone stamped my stack of books and Isabella's one. I always got a stack, and Isabella always got just one. She would keep it in her purse, so, she told me, she could read it on the bus in the morning, and sometimes she would read bits and pieces to me.

I was helping Isabella get Jesse's carriage up the steps when it hit me that there was one special thing I wanted. "I don't guess you have any books with music written in them, do you?" I asked Miss Perone.

"We have a couple of guitar books." She was already heading for the music section, and I was behind her.

"No, I mean for piano."

"Not much," she said. She pulled out a long, red book. "We do have this one on folk songs."

"That's good," I said.

Isabella and I sat on the front steps waiting for Mama. I sat Jesse on my lap. He looked up and down and around, like he was watching out for Mama. "Pamela Tucker's already finished with Miss Love's book," I said.

Isabella took my hand and smiled. "You know, we shouldn't keep Pamela Tucker a secret from your mama the way we do."

"Mama never asked me anything about Pamela." People on Brown Street weren't real happy with those Tucker kids; they were always coming into people's yards, causing trouble. Pamela Tucker didn't do anything, but people didn't take notice of which particular Tucker it was causing the trouble.

Isabella shook her head. "We think about it, Rachel. We're careful not to mention it. It's the same as lying."

I could see our car turning the corner. "Yes ma'am."

"I'm not blaming you, in any way. I encouraged the deception. It was my fault."

"But — "

Mama pulled up in front of us and waved.

"You do understand, don't you?"

"Yes ma'am."

"So what you got today?" Mama asked.

"A music book and — "

"For the piano?"

"Yes ma'am."

"Well, that's wonderful that you're as interested as all that."

I tried to see the title of Isabella's book, but the way it was stuck in her purse, I could only make out the last part of the writer's name. Baldwin.

I didn't see Pamela Tucker until Tuesday after my piano lesson.

"Good afternoon, Pamela," Miss Love said because, of course, she had wondered about the girl always waiting outside when she left and had asked me her name.

"Hello, Miss Love," Pamela Tucker said. She said it real nice, but rolled her eyes at me behind her back. "Love?" she had asked me. "Love?" She couldn't believe there was really a person with that name.

Curt Tucker stood in the middle of the road and wouldn't move out from in front of Miss Love's car. Finally, she blew the horn, and, knowing Miss Love the way I did, I knew she hated to make that loud noise. "Can't you make him move?"

Pamela Tucker shook her head. "I don't want them to know I come over here." She stood up and slipped inside the screen door.

Curt Tucker walked, very slowly, to the curb. Miss Love nodded, very nicely, to him as she drove by. It made me so mad. Just the same, I went inside and sat down on the bench with Pamela. I had to agree with her, about just ignoring it, because I sure didn't want to have to deal with Curt Tucker up close. "Guess what?" I said.

"What?" Pamela Tucker didn't look at me. She just sat on the piano stool and flipped ahead in the book.

"We picked out my recital piece today."

She jerked around and gave me those snake eyes. "What does that mean?"

Anybody else talking to me the way Pamela Tucker did would make me cry. I guess I just didn't hear her anymore. "There's going to be a recital, in May, when we play in front of our parents, and so I have to learn 'The Waltz of the Stars' by heart. That's my song."

"That one's easy."

"I have to learn it by heart," I said. "I have to play it without looking."

"What's this?" she said. She pulled the library book out from behind the music rack.

"I got that at the library."

"Yeah?" She looked surprised. She flipped through it and settled on a song called "This Land Is Your Land." She picked it out, singing bits here and there. "We sang this in school once before," she said.

I nodded.

"That library, it's down in the courthouse, right?"

"Yeah," I said. "Don't you go there?"

Pamela Tucker shook her head. "My daddy, he said . . . well, you got to be a member and all, right?"

I shrugged. "They do give you a card, but it doesn't cost anything. It's real easy."

"What do you do?"

"Well, I just filled out my name and address, and then got my Mama to sign it, and — "

Pamela Tucker slammed the book down. "Well," she said, "just forget it then."

I picked it up. "Why don't you take it for a while, look it over. It's too hard for me."

"Why'd you get it then?"

I shrugged. "Just remember, I got to take it back in a couple of weeks."

"Don't you dare!" Pamela screamed. She jumped, so I grabbed onto the keyboard to keep from falling back.

Curt Tucker was standing at our front door, sticking out his tongue. Pamela lit out after him, holding the book over her head, like she was going to hit him. He ran.

"Don't you tell him!" Pamela yelled.

Isabella came in from the kitchen. "What's all that?" she said.

We watched them run into the white house. "Now that was a library book she had," I said. "Checked out in my name."

Isabella patted my head. We stood there a minute, watching the white house, and I figured Miss Peaks was standing at her kitchen window, trying to see what all the commotion in our house was about.

Thirteen

It wasn't me that brought up Scout camp with Mama, it was Aunt Celeste. It seemed that Florence, a lady she knew from the shop, was sending her little girl. "They all do it," Aunt Celeste said. "I think it would be real good for Rachel to go."

I was just about to go into the kitchen with them, but I hung back to hear how that conversation was going to go.

"It's not as if I'm keeping her from it, Celeste," Mama said. "This is the first I've heard of it."

That was as far as it went because that wasn't what Aunt Celeste had come over to talk about. But at least now I wouldn't have to bring up the subject with Mama, she'd bring it up with me.

What Aunt Celeste really wanted to talk about was Uncle Carter and Macy Mitchell. "I think they're up to something," she said.

"Like what?"

"I think they're seriously thinking about getting married."

"About time."

I went into the kitchen. Everyone seemed to like Macy Mitchell well enough. Everyone, except for Grandma Graham, seemed to think Uncle Carter needed a girlfriend or a wife or something, so I figured this was happy news. As soon as I saw Aunt Celeste's pinched lips and staring eyes, I knew I had been wrong.

"She's divorced," Aunt Celeste said.

"Well, for heaven's sake, Celeste. I know that."

"Maybe she's the wrong sort of woman for Carter."

"Because she's divorced?"

I slid up on the stool at the counter. Neither one of them took any notice.

"I don't mean it in a bad way. It's just that . . . Carter's led a sheltered life."

"One thing he hasn't been sheltered from is divorce." Mama was mad. "He grew up without a daddy just like you and me."

"Well, yeah." Celeste looked up and seemed surprised to see me. "True enough."

"Well, you come on over tomorrow, too."

"Okay."

They could do that, Mama and Celeste; get mad and make up in the next minute.

That night I lay awake and listened to Mama relay the whole conversation to Daddy. "More power to them," he said. Mama repeated conversations she had with other people to Daddy, and he would have something to say about it, just as if he'd been able to be there. Mama acted things so well that Daddy thought he was in on more things than he was. You could tell by the way he talked later, as if he'd actually been there.

The next afternoon, just like Aunt Celeste said, Uncle Carter and Macy showed up at our house.

The wedding was going to be in July because they could both get away from their work at that time. They wanted to spend a few days in Charleston after the wedding.

"I hear it's lovely there," Mama said.

"It's going to be hot, in July like that," Aunt Celeste said.

"But still lovely," Mama said. She shook her head at Aunt Celeste. "You going to be married at Central Presbyterian?" That was Grandma Graham and Uncle Carter's church. When we went, we went to the Baptist church.

"We've decided to have a garden wedding."

Mama and Aunt Celeste looked at each other. Aunt Celeste and Macy both lived in apartments. Mama laughed. "We don't have much of a garden, Macy."

"Oh, we're going to have it at Miss Graham's."

Mama and Aunt Celeste looked at each other. Jesse, who was lounging on his blanket in the middle of the floor, flipped over and laughed, so everyone else laughed, too. It was the first sound I'd heard out of Uncle Carter all afternoon.

Uncle Carter and Macy offered to give Aunt Celeste a ride home, but she said no, she thought she would visit for a while. "I think Mama likes Macy," she said when they were out the door.

"Maybe she just realized there's nothing she can do about it."

Aunt Celeste leaned down and picked up Jesse. She leaned back with him in the pink chair. "No," she said. "I think she really likes her."

Mama thought it over. "Maybe because she's divorced, maybe she feels for what she went through."

"Maybe."

"As I understand it, it was a lot like Daddy, just up and gone one day, never to return. Maybe Mama — "

"Well," Aunt Celeste said, "Daddy returned. He was just a little late."

Mama stared at her.

Aunt Celeste wasn't paying attention. "That could be it, you know, because I never saw Mama more cold and wicked than she was that day. He wanted to know how to get to you, he knew about Rachel, but — "

"What day?" Mama said. Jesse started whimpering, so Aunt Celeste handed him off to her. "What are you talking about?"

Aunt Celeste sat up straight. She went pale. "Well, he did come by, but Mama got rid of him right away.

She said not to say anything, but I just figured she would or — "

"Well, you figured wrong," Mama said. They leaned back and stared each other down. Mama had cried two years ago when she got the letter saying the daddy she'd gotten her red hair and freckles from was dead. She'd called him names, but she'd cried.

"Mama told him you hated him," Aunt Celeste said. "She said you wouldn't want to see him, not after all this time, not after nothing for all those years."

"You want to ride with me to take Aunt Celeste home?" There were tears in Mama's eyes.

"No ma'am," I said. "I could stay here and watch Jesse."

She nodded and handed Jesse off to me. He was having a great time.

Fourteen

Pamela Tucker learned "Nearer My God to Thee" out of the hymnal and played it for Isabella. She wanted to teach me some of those folk songs out of the library book, at least the right-hand part, but all I could think about was "The Waltz of the Stars." I had to play it and play it to learn it by heart, until my fingers were so sore that they wouldn't go any way but the right way. I was going to play the piano in front of people. Mama, Grandma Graham and Aunt Celeste were going to come. Daddy, of course, would have to work; they couldn't both be away from the store at the same time. Isabella said I'd have to give her a private recital in my new dress, as if she didn't hear me play "The Waltz of the Stars" over and over again every day. I even caught her humming it sometimes.

"You want to see the dress I'm going to wear to the recital?" I asked Pamela Tucker.

"I guess so," she said. Sometimes Pamela Tucker came in the back door, through our kitchen, but other than that she was always at the piano. She'd never been in my room before.

"I probably wouldn't have gotten a new dress just for the recital, but my uncle's getting married, and I'm wearing it to his wedding, too."

She nodded and sat on my bed. "This is a nice room."

I waited for the nasty remark to come after that, but it didn't. "Yeah." I looked around. "It really is nice." I thought that might sound snobby. "I didn't have my own room before we moved here."

"You moved here from somewhere else?"

I hoped she wouldn't notice that I could watch her house from my window. Some nights it got loud over there. "We used to live in an apartment, behind my father's store."

"Where'd you live before that?"

"That's all. Just the store, and then we moved here."

"I've lived in ten different places, and I won't even be thirteen until next month."

Isabella knocked on the door. She had cookies. She was smiling.

"So let me see the dress," Pamela Tucker said. "We don't want your mother to show up and find me here. She might have a fit." She took a bite of a cookie. Isabella had offered her something to eat every time she came by, but this was the first time she'd ever accepted.

111

I pulled the dress out of the closet. "I don't like it," she said. "It's too grownup-looking for you." She wiped the crumbs off her hands.

Mama had said pretty much the same thing. She didn't like it at all, but she had made the mistake of getting carried away and saying that I could pick out the dress all by myself. She had said, "It doesn't do a thing for you." But she had promised, and it was on a clearance rack — ten dollars cheaper than the dresses she liked.

"Try it on," Pamela Tucker said.

I did. It was the first time I'd had it on since the store, and I could see that what had been worrying me was true. I didn't like it, either. Not anymore. "The material's real pretty, don't you think?"

"Yeah, it's good." Pamela fingered the pink-and-red-flowered cotton, but she sat back up and shook her head. "But those crisscrosses in the back and that squared-off neck — it's like you're supposed to have something, and you don't. You're just a kid."

"There's a sweater that goes with it," I said. "It's nice." I took it off the hanger and gave it to Pamela.

"Ooooh," she said. "It's beautiful."

"And what the heck is this?" Mama had said, holding it up by the shoulders. It was a short, round pink sweater, held together by one pink pearl button. Little swirls of pink and rose pearls were sewn on the front. "I've never seen anything like it," I said. "Except in the movies."

112

"I love it," Pamela said. She looked at me. "I take it all back."

Isabella knocked on the door again. She had Jesse on her hip. "Your mother's out front, Rachel."

I couldn't believe it was six already.

"Bye," Pamela said and headed out the back through the kitchen.

"Oh, that door's locked," Isabella said. "Come out front with us."

Pamela looked at me.

"Come on," I said.

Isabella, Jesse and I got in the car. Mama stared after Pamela walking down the street. "Who is that?"

"Pamela Tucker," I said.

"She was teaching Rachel something on the piano," Isabella said.

"Tucker?" Mama said. "Those Tuckers?" She pointed at the white house. "She plays the piano?"

"Yes ma'am," I said.

Mama shook her head as if she didn't know what the world was coming to.

Isabella smiled at me.

When we arrived at Miss Love's at seven o'clock on the evening of May twenty-third, Mama, Aunt Celeste and Grandma Graham were taken by Miss Love's sister, the other Miss Love, into the living room, and I was taken into the bedroom to wait my turn to perform. There were five of us; Marcia, Susan and Catherine had been taking from Miss Love a long time, and it was Kevin's first time, just like me.

We could hear the other Miss Love passing out punch, while our Miss Love explained that something always happened at a recital that you hadn't expected. "Usually," she said, "it's just a little thing, something that keeps things fun, but last year a young lady — "

"Patty Keenan," Marcia hissed at me and Kevin.

"She had actually been in an earlier recital, with only the normal amount of nervousness, but last year — "

Marcia, Susan and Catherine all looked at Kevin and me and nodded.

"She was overcome by terror, she fell from the stool, she ripped her lovely little blue dress, she — "

Marcia and Susan cringed. Catherine stuck out her tongue. Kevin and I leaned closer to the partly opened bedroom door.

"She not only never took another piano lesson, she told her mother she hated music, that she never wanted to sit before the keyboard again." Miss Love clapped her hands. Her voice rose up and happy with her next words. "But I have made arrangements this year which I'm sure will leave everyone, parents and children alike, happy and satisfied."

"She vomited," Marcia hissed at us. "It got all over my mother's shoes."

The arrangement was that we played our recital pieces, all alone, staring at ourselves in the mirror hanging behind the piano in the dining room. Our parents smiled and listened and stared at the green walls of the living room. I could see why Miss Love thought it was better — it wasn't as scary, not being able to see any people, just being in the room with the piano — but it was a disappointment.

Pamela Tucker said it was the stupidest thing she'd ever heard of, and she was glad she had no part of it.

Fifteen

Summer came all of a sudden, with it getting real hot and the Tuckers going wild all in one week. Mr. Tucker smashed a car parked on the street. At first he said he didn't do it — it had happened late at night — but he didn't bother to hide his own smashed pickup. Miss Peaks told Isabella he made a deal to work off the damage at the guy's garage. One night Mr. Haynes called the police about the screams coming from the white house. Mama and I watched from my bedroom window, but the police didn't take anyone away. Curt Tucker broke out a window in the house across the street. Miss Peaks said she heard they were going to make good on it, but that he had done it deliberately, with a big grin on his face.

"That child needs some serious attention," Miss Peaks said.

"Yes ma'am, he does," Isabella said.

Mama and Daddy even talked about the Tuckers at night. "This street is being overrun by hooligans," Mama said.

"It's not the kids," Daddy said. "That family's boiling over from the top down."

"Well, whatever the reason, something's got to be done."

"Put one of those air conditioning units in their window," Daddy said. "That'd take care of it."

"Everybody's hot, Fred. That doesn't give us license to run wild."

Mama kept an eye out for the Tuckers when she was around, but she never did tie Pamela Tucker in with all the trouble. I figured it was just that she trusted Isabella's judgment.

Miss Love stopped giving lessons during summer vacation, but Pamela Tucker didn't stop coming over at the regular time. She didn't come to the front door anymore, though; she always came around back, over the fence and through the back door into the kitchen. She knew how things were. She was jumpy. "What's she looking at?" she said, hunching down.

"She's just looking." Isabella waved to Miss Peaks through the window. "We just happen to be here."

"Can I play your piano?" Pamela Tucker said.

"I'm eating," I said. "You want some crackers?"

She shook her head. "I don't need you."

"Go ahead." I rolled my eyes at Isabella. She gave me that little nod that meant I was supposed to just overlook it.

Jesse banged on his high-chair tray, so I gave him another piece of graham cracker. Pamela started in on a song from my book, one called Hungarian something or other. I'd played it for Miss Love, but with Pamela playing, it was like hearing it for the first time. Quick and sharp. Isabella smiled and folded towels and put them into the basket in time to the music. Jesse clapped his hands together.

"Did you see that?" I asked Isabella.

She smiled. "He likes music."

Pamela Tucker started in on another one. It sounded as if she was just moving through the book, song by song.

"Are you going to miss school?" Isabella said.

I shook my head.

"I thought you liked school."

"Everybody thinks that," I said, "but I get tired of it."

"Of the work?"

I shook my head. "Sometimes I like to just think, off to myself, just for a minute, and in school, they don't like you doing that."

Isabella shrugged. "Plenty of time for that now."

I shrugged. "Well, I wish Miss Love didn't stop music lessons just because it was summer, and I wish camp would start up."

"Well now, you just take this extra time, off to yourself, and get some of that thinking done."

"I guess." I did patty-cake with Jesse. He knew exactly how to do it now.

Isabella finished with her towels. "I'll put those away later, when we come back tonight," I said.

She winked. She sat down and ate one of the graham crackers. Pamela Tucker went through another song. "Does Pamela ever talk about the others, about little Curt?"

"No," I said. "Like what?"

"I wonder why he's so troubled."

Just like Isabella believed there was never a reason for being untruthful, she believed there was good in everybody. I wasn't going to argue with her, because it wouldn't come to anything, but if I had to come up with two things I'd learned for sure in school, it would be that Isabella was wrong on those counts. "He just likes to be bad."

"No," Isabella said. She wiped Jesse's mouth and took him out to check his diaper. "Uh-oh." She patted my head on her way out. "Tell Pamela she'd better wrap things up."

I'd always start fidgeting, thinking of something else, and have to get up from the piano before too long, but I think Pamela Tucker could have hunched over those piano keys until the end of time without going anywhere else. "I got to leave?" she asked.

"Not right this minute," I said. "Finish what you were playing." She started up again, and I stood behind her, following along with the notes as she played. I'd never done that before. I hadn't even realized that I could. Pamela Tucker got to the end, then started all over from the beginning. "You're playing it again."

She gave me the quick snake eyes, but kept right on playing until she was ready to stop. "Don't you know how to read music?"

"Yeah," I said. "That's how I know you started all over again."

"What do you think those two dots right there mean?"

"I don't know."

She turned back several pages. "Well, it tells you right here, in your own book." She pointed at the dots on the top of the page. "Repeat," it said after the dots. "It means repeat. Play it again until you come to the double bars — " She turned back to the piece she'd been playing. "See right here. That's where I stopped the second time."

"Oh yeah," I said. I thought maybe I did remember hearing something about that.

"Bye." Pamela Tucker went through the kitchen to the door. "Bye," she said to Isabella.

"Wait and go out with us," Isabella said.

Pamela Tucker shook her head.

"You can come back and play," I said.

"Yeah. Maybe."

I watched her climb over the fence, then went back to the piano to look for more songs with dots and double bars.

Sixteen

We had to fill out papers to let them know I was coming to camp. You could buy camp T-shirts to wear every day or just wear plain shorts and shirts. Mama said she didn't see much sense in special outfits to wear for two short weeks. I didn't either. I tried to call Caroline to talk about camp, but could never get an answer. She had probably gone to Panama City Beach like last year.

Mama let me out in the parking lot at the top of a hill, and I followed the other kids down into a flat pit with an American flag twenty times bigger than the one at school. On the other side was a hill full of woods, but a tall blond lady with a deep voice told us to stay down under the flag. She gave us each white envelopes called orientation packets. I saw Caroline and Cynthia up on the hill; they got out of the same car. Something about the way they skipped down the hill, holding hands, made me feel funny — I'd never seen them do that before. They waved and skipped right over to me, but the blond lady stepped in front of them. "Ho!" she said. "Hold on there, girls." She gave them their orientation packets and moved on.

Caroline pulled the papers out of the envelope. A few of them fell on the ground, and Cynthia and I helped catch them before they blew away. "Hey," Caroline said when she had them stuffed back in the envelope. "We just got back from the beach last night." She was very brown and wearing one of the special T-shirts.

"That's neat," I said. Daddy said that one day, and one day soon, he was just going to close up, maybe even for a whole week, and we were going to go to the beach. I wanted to ask exactly what the ocean was like, but I knew they would think it was weird that I'd never been.

Cynthia's nose was peeling. She was wearing one of the T-shirts, too. "We would have been here on time, but Caroline wouldn't get up."

"Nothing's happened yet," I said.

The blond lady and all the big girls wearing green shirts formed us into a horseshoe — that's what they called it — and led us in our pledge, motto and prayer. They divided us into ten groups. The big girls stepped out and read their lists of names; if you were on it, you had to go stand behind that girl. Caroline and Cynthia were in my line. There had been a line on the papers we filled out that asked if there were any particular friends you would like in your group. Since

Caroline was going to be my buddy — she'd brought it up every single Scout meeting — I had put her. Since it wouldn't be nice not to put Cynthia, I had put her, too. Callie Thompson and Sandra Collins from our troop were in the line, too, but all the rest of the kids I didn't know. These Scouts came from all over the county.

They marched our groups up into the woods; one green-shirt girl led the way and another walked behind us. Halfway up we could see the lake. Caroline pulled on my shirt. I nodded. I had my lunch and bathing suit and towel in a little satchel like most everybody else, but Callie Thompson was wearing hers in a back-pack. That made a lot of sense, walking around the way we were in the woods. I decided to check and see if we had something like that around the house. Daddy probably had one put away somewhere.

"My name is Sharon," the first green-shirt girl said. "And this is Kay." She pointed to the other green-shirt girl. Kay waved to us. Sharon told us we were patrol #7, but that we would vote on our own special name a little later. She told us that we'd be doing crafts and swimming and maybe going out in a canoe.

"The most important thing to making our patrol productive and fun," Kay said, "is the buddy system."

I turned around and tried to catch Caroline's eye, but she was looking up into the tops of the trees.

"What that means is you always have a partner to help you out and know where you are," Sharon said.

"We're here for all of you," Kay said.

"But," Sharon said, "we're really just backup for your buddy. If you've already picked out a buddy, get together and find a spot for your own special little camp."

"The rest of you mill around, get to know each other, and we'll help pair you up if you want."

I saw Caroline point out a thick tree at the edge of our roped-out area and Cynthia follow her over. "You and me, we'll be buddies." If she'd said it once, she'd said it a thousand times. I bit my lip to keep the tears from coming. She had forgotten. I turned right smack into Callie Thompson's face. "You want to be my buddy?" I said.

"Yes," she said. She pointed to a couple of small trees. "That's the best place." I followed her up. "See how they come together to form a kind of chair. We could take turns sitting on it. And look." I followed her finger. "There's moss." She hung her backpack on a branch. I set my satchel on the ground. "Hang it up here," Callie said. "Ants might get in it." I moved it. "Now," she said in a whisper, "I heard there's not enough boats for everybody. We have to sign up to get in one. So if you get down to the lake first, sign our names on the paper tacked up beside the dock."

"How do you know that?"

"I just heard. I checked around, found out what's what."

"I'd just as soon swim."

Callie glared at me. "We can get our boating badge."

The girl didn't let up.

When Mama picked me up on Friday of the first week Sharon leaned into the car and said, "I just want to tell you what a wonderful little girl you have. All of us, but you know, especially Kay and me, we were worried to death about what was going to happen with Callie, her being the only one and all — we'd never had this situation before — but little Rachel here, she was so great, she just saved the day." She put her hand on Mama's shoulder. "I just wanted to let you know."

"Well, thank you very much," Mama said. She flashed her big store smile. "What on earth was she talking about?" she asked me.

"I don't know." My shoulders burned, I was tired and I didn't feel like talking.

"I see my threat worked."

"What?"

"I see you did manage to get your hair up again after swimming."

"Callie did it. I told her what you said, that you were going to cut all my hair off, in a pixie." I spit that word out the window. Pixie.

"I didn't say it to be mean. I thought it would be easier for you to manage."

"She said it wasn't my fault. She said it was the way my hair was, so fine and slippery, that made it hard for me to get it back up. She said it would be awful mean to cut off my hair."

"Who said this now? One of the counselors?"

"No. Callie. Callie Thompson. My buddy."

"Callie Thompson." Mama took her eyes off the road. "Isn't that the little Negro girl from the school?"

"Yes ma'am."

"I thought you were all set with that Caroline."

"Yeah." I stared out the window. I wasn't over it. "She forgot."

"Oh."

"I'm glad. Me and Callie, we've been taking out the canoe instead of swimming some days. We're going to get our boating badge."

"Well, you better be swimming every chance you get. It's going to be a hot summer, and I don't know — "

"Me and Callie, we've got more badges than anybody in the whole troop."

Mama pulled up in front of the house. "Did she ask you to be her . . . her . . ."

"Buddy?"

"Yeah. Did she ask you?"

"No, I asked her."

"Well, now, I see what the girl was carrying on about. A lot of little girls, even if they liked the little Negro — "

"Callie doesn't like being called that."

"Well, what does she — ?"

126

"I don't know. Just girl."

Mama shook her head. "Well, all right. What I mean is, it was good of you to realize this Callie was a good partner, just like anybody else." That's pretty much what Sharon had whispered to me. "She's really no different than anyone else," she'd said.

It was four-thirty by the time we got home, but Mama said she had to go back to the store anyway. She'd be back at six to pick Isabella up.

"You look tired," Isabella said.

"Yes ma'am, I am," I said.

"Well, go back to your room and rest a while," she said, "just as soon as you rinse out that bathing suit."

I held it under the faucet for a minute, then hung it over the shower rod. I was really tired. I pushed my head down into the coolness of my pillow.

Pamela Tucker barged into my room. "She says I got to ask, so can I?"

"Yeah." I didn't open my eyes.

"What's wrong with you?"

"I'm tired. I been at camp."

"Yeah? Can you swim?"

"Sort of."

"I had a cousin drown," she said. "I didn't really know him, but they told me about it."

"They got lifeguards. And then you got your buddy — you know, your camp partner — and you're always watching out for each other, too."

"Who's yours? That loud little girl?"

"No." I knew right away she meant Caroline. "Callie Thompson."

"You're kidding."

"No."

"Sue told me about her. She's the nig — " Pamela looked up. She'd left my door open. "She's the colored girl."

Callie hadn't said anything, but I could tell she didn't like that word either. "Yeah."

"Why you stuck with her?"

"She's no different than anybody else."

Pamela Tucker snorted. "That's real nice." She turned her head. "That's the nicest thing you can say? That she's just regular, nothing special, nothing out of the ordinary." Pamela walked out. "Oh, that's real nice."

I listened to her first song, but when Isabella woke me up at six, Pamela Tucker was already gone.

The second Monday of camp we were late. Mama had to get out of the car and clean the terminals, but finally the car started up. All the way she grumbled. "Your father's just going to have to do something about this car. I can't put up with this aggravation, not on top of everything else." When we pulled into the parking lot, the horseshoe was already formed. "See you this afternoon," Mama said.

"I don't think I should go down now," I said. "It

wouldn't be respectful to break in on prayer and pledging and all that." Kids did it, but I didn't think it was right.

"It doesn't matter," Mama said. "I've got to go to the bank. Hop out and move down real quiet."

I got out, but sat at the top of the hill when she pulled away. I couldn't recognize anybody. Most of them were wearing those same T-shirts. They all came together in one long, pale, unrecognizable thread, all except for Callie Thompson. I knew her, sticking out like one black, shiny knot in the thread, and I knew what Pamela Tucker was trying to say. Who was I, and who were Sharon and Kay and Mama, to say to somebody like Callie Thompson, "You're just as good as us." Maybe she was better. Maybe she didn't want to be like us. It was a stuck-up thing to say.

I hadn't told Mama everything. Callie had said it would be terrible if Mama cut my hair into a pixie, but she had also said that if she did, it would be my own fault. "You knew your head was a mess. You knew your mama didn't like it. If you couldn't do anything about it, you should have asked someone who could. You got to do what you got to do." She was sort of like a preacher, but Callie Thompson wasn't like any kid I'd ever known.

Pamela Tucker was right. If you were going to say anything about her at all, that was the thing to say, that she was different from everybody else.

129

Seventeen

Now that I'd seen Miss Peaks's garden, I knew that what Grandma Graham had wasn't a garden. It was a flower farm. There were no benches or fountains, no colonnades and curves, just rows and rows of irises, lilies, roses and sunflowers. Grandma Graham didn't sit and drink tea with her flowers, she worked them and harvested them, just like tomatoes and corn, to supply her church on Sundays, and weddings and funerals, and we always had flowers on our dining room table. She was famous for her African violets. One wall of her living room was filled with rows and rows of pots on high shelves, but you didn't visit with them the way Miss Peaks visited her English landscape garden. It was more like a scientist's laboratory.

Still, once Aunt Celeste had hosed down the side porch and Macy Mitchell had arranged the folded chairs borrowed from the funeral home, I could see how the flowers would make a real pretty background for a wedding. That was all done by the time Mama went over after work to help, but there was still plenty to do.

Aunt Celeste filled a tray of tiny pink paper cups with nuts. Macy mixed orange-strawberry punch in gallon jars. Mama made slow, wide circles on the dining table. Grandma sat in her rocker with her hands folded in her lap.

"I know you girls think I'm just awful, sitting here, watching you do all the work, but these old bones have just about given up," Grandma said.

"We told you we'd take care of it," Mama said.

"Don't you worry about anything, Miss Graham," Macy said.

"Well, it is my house," Grandma said.

The smells of Grandma's house — the violets, the sachets, the cedar, and especially the lemon stuff Mama was rubbing into the table — settled thick around my head.

"Rachel, run into the bedroom and check to see if Jesse's still asleep," Mama said.

"I can't." I was so tired.

They all looked up. "What?" Mama said.

"She's tired," Aunt Celeste said. "She ought to be in bed herself."

"What time is it?" Mama said.

"Ten-thirty."

"Take them home, Bobbie. We're pretty much finished anyway," Macy Mitchell said.

"It's not as if it's that big a deal," Aunt Celeste said.

Macy Mitchell looked at her.

"Well," Aunt Celeste said, "what I mean is that we're just setting up for twenty people, twenty people that are family or might as well be, so — "

"I don't know about your family," Macy said, "but even though some of mine are good as gold, most of them are just looking for something to talk about."

"Well, it's not as if it'll be any reflection on you," Grandma Graham said. "It is my house, after all."

Mama said, "Well, I think it's shaping up just fine." She went into the bedroom to get Jesse.

"Look at those windows." Grandma Graham smiled. "First time Carter's cleaned them outside in ten years. They do sparkle."

Mama came back with Jesse asleep on her shoulder. "Come on, Rachel. We don't want you falling asleep during the ceremony tomorrow."

"The heck with it," Macy said. "I say we're ready."

"Yeah," Aunt Celeste said. "A bride's got to get her beauty sleep, after all."

"Come on, Rachel," Mama said. She was waiting at the door with Jesse. She looked so far away. I stood up and vomited all over Grandma Graham's heirloom rag rug. I looked at them, all just standing there, looking at me.

Aunt Celeste was the first to react. She went into the bathroom and brought back a wet cloth for my face, but she didn't bring it to me; she took Jesse from

132

Mama and gave the cloth to her. Mama helped me over to a vinyl kitchen chair — one that could be sponged off — and wiped my face. "Why didn't you tell me you were sick?" she said.

"I didn't know."

"Just hold this on your face," she said. She bent over and folded the rug. "I'll wash the rug out in the bathtub, hang it out right now and it'll be fine for tomorrow."

Grandma Graham pushed herself up out of her rocker. "I'll do that," she said. "Get that poor child home and into her own bed."

"It'll just take a minute," Mama said.

"Bobbie," Grandma said, "the poor child's falling out of the chair."

"Okay." Mama put her arm around my shoulder. Aunt Celeste carried Jesse out to the car.

"Tell Miss Mitchell I'm sorry," I said.

"Don't be silly, dear," Aunt Celeste said. "You get some rest, and I'll see you tomorrow."

I woke up the next morning tired and heavy. Mama took one look at me and called the doctor. I sat up to see myself in the mirror. My face was fat, and it was sore. The doctor told Mama she could bring me in if she wanted, but he could tell her right over the telephone that I had the mumps. I couldn't go to the wedding. I didn't even want to get up and brush my teeth.

"I don't guess you could stay just a little longer, could you, Isabella, just until I get back from the wedding?"

Isabella only worked half days on Saturday. "Oh, Miss Bobbie," Isabella said. "I wish more than anything that I could, but we've got people down from Pennsylvania for a church meeting, and I have to be there."

"What time's your meeting? I could zip right out, skip the to-do, and be back before four-thirty."

Isabella bit her lip and said, "I could call my brother, Miss Bobbie, and maybe see if we could meet a little later, but I do have to be there."

"Great," Mama said. "I'm going to run to the store real quick. You feel like apple juice, Rachel?"

"No ma'am." I could hear Isabella on the phone.

"Well, okay, Gary, I know. I just told Miss Bobbie I'd ask." She was quiet for a long time. "It was unexpected, that's all, kind of an emergency." More quiet, then, "Okay. I told her I'd ask, and that's all I'm doing. Asking." She came into my room and kissed me. "Do you need anything?" I shook my head. She stood staring out the window, in the direction of the white house, biting her lip.

Mama came home with the apple juice and Grandma Graham. They were arguing. "How on earth is Carter going to feel if you're not at the wedding?"

"It won't make a whit of difference. He has my blessing. What more does he want?"

"Mama, this is silly. Isabella's going to stay just a little longer, so — "

"That poor girl's worked all week long. Let her go home, and I'll stay here with the children."

Mama threw up her hands. "This is crazy." She went into the kitchen and told Isabella, "She's got her mind set. You want to go on home now? Then I could just dash back and get dressed."

"Miss Bobbie, why don't I just take the bus?"

"For goodness sake, no," Mama said.

"One will be along in ten minutes or so."

"You don't mind?"

"No ma'am. It's not too hot out. There's a nice breeze."

"Well." Mama thought it over. "It is broad daylight, so I guess . . . You just go on whenever you're ready."

Isabella came in a little while later and kissed me good-bye. "I love you," she said. "Get better." She looked real happy. I knew how she felt. She was leaving, and Mama thought it was her idea. It was like me going to camp without even having to ask, without any effort at all.

Mama dressed up in her aquamarine knit dress and black patent-leather high heels and put Jesse down for his nap. Grandma Graham smiled in on me for a few

135

minutes after Mama left, as if she'd never liked me better in my life. Then she went into the living room, found her radio station and settled back in the rocking chair. I pushed down snug and sore in my bed.

I opened my eyes. Pamela Tucker was tapping on the window. Isabella wasn't here, I had the mumps and Jesse was sleeping. She couldn't play the piano today. She had on big silver hoop earrings and a red scarf wrapped around her neck. I looked right at her and didn't make a move. She tapped fast and low. Grandma was snoring in the living room, so I opened the window.

"I'm sick," I said.

"Yeah, I saw your mama leave without you."

"You can't play today. I'm sick, and my grandma's here."

"Listen, I just came to say good-bye. My dad is in some kind of trouble, I don't know, but anyway, we're leaving."

I sat up. "What do you mean?"

Pamela pushed up the window and climbed in. "Boy, you look awful."

"I've got the mumps."

"Yeah, I had those," Pamela said. "Your ears hurt?"

I nodded. "Where are you going?"

Pamela shrugged. "I don't know. We don't ever go far."

"For how long?"

Pamela looked at me as if I'd just asked what double dots meant. "Forever. They're packing up, and we're going."

"You can't just up and move all of a sudden like that."

She shrugged. "We do it all the time."

I didn't know what to say.

"I got to go this time," she said, "but I got me a part-time job, down in Dickersons' Ice Cream Shop, and I'm saving up my money." She gave me a striped handkerchief folded into a little bundle. "Next time they can go without me. Next time I'm striking out on my own. I'm going off and be a movie star."

I unfolded the handkerchief. Inside were her drop pearl earrings. "I know you're too little for these now, but I wanted to give you something. I liked playing your piano," Pamela Tucker said.

"I liked you playing it, too."

"Tell Isabella bye for me. She's real nice."

"Yeah."

Jesse let out a yell. Grandma Graham's snoring jerked to a stop. "Bye," Pamela whispered.

"Wait," I hissed back. I got out of bed and pulled the pink sweater off my dress. "You have this." Pamela was taller than me, but skinnier in the arms.

"No," she said.

"Yeah," I said.

"You want something, Rachel?" Grandma Graham called from the living room.

"No ma'am." Pamela Tucker pushed through the window. I grabbed my library card off the dresser. "This, too," I said.

She reached for it, looked it over and shook her head. "It's got your name on it. It won't do me any good."

"Try it," I said. My ear was aching. I squeezed the pearl earrings in my hand.

Grandma Graham came in and sat on the end of my bed. Jesse watched from the door; he didn't hang on her the way he did on Isabella. "Your mama left a big jug of apple juice. You want some of that?"

"No ma'am."

"There's a can of chicken rice soup in there."

"No ma'am. I feel like I might be sick again."

Grandma laughed. "Well, no, we sure don't want that mess." She shook her head. "Did you see the look on that girl's face?"

"Who?"

"Why, Miss Macy Mitchell."

"I think I'll sleep some more."

"I might have some of that soup myself, so if you change your mind — "

"Jesse likes it," I said. "He'll eat some." I turned to the wall, careful to keep my hand with the earrings under the cover. "Night."

Grandma patted my head. "Well, honey, it's too bad you're sick, but I sure am happy to have a reason to be here rather than over there at the wedding."

I heard Mama when she came in from the wedding. I woke up again and saw Mama and Daddy standing over me, whispering. It kept up all the night, the waking up, the going back to sleep, and each time I woke up I was more tired than the time before. When I really and truly woke up late Sunday morning there was a piece of toast with three bites taken out of it. I could almost remember eating it. It was like a dream.

The next morning Isabella came in and opened my blinds. She stared for a moment at the white house. "I made eggs," she said. "You want to get up to eat, or do you want them in here?"

"I'll get up," I said, but I was slow about it, and I think I made a groaning face, so Isabella brought a tray into the bedroom anyway.

"You been suffering much?"

"No ma'am, mostly just tired. And I look funny."

Isabella opened the window. "It's a beautiful day out."

The eggs were good. "Boy, I'm hungry," I said. "I was scared the whole time to eat, scared I was going to get sick again, but I think I'm over that now because last night I had some potatoes and — "

"Rachel?"

"Yes ma'am?"

"I think the Tuckers are gone."

I put the tray on the end of the bed and climbed out to look with her. The FOR RENT sign was back in front of the white house. The windows were naked. "Yes ma'am. Pamela Tucker said to tell you good-bye."

Isabella looked at me. "When did you see Pamela Tucker?"

"She came to the window."

Jesse cried out. Isabella went to see about him.

I dug under the covers until I found my pearl earrings; they'd worked their way down to the bottom and were still wrapped in the handkerchief. Pamela Tucker was gone, but for the first time I knew that just like Caroline had Cynthia, and Cynthia had Caroline, I had Pamela Tucker. She was my secret and certain and forever best friend.

I finished my book, ate a little chicken broth for lunch, drank some juice and took a nap. Maybe I was dreaming about Pamela or the library or Miss Perone or something, but I woke up calling out to Isabella to help me find the number to the library. "I let Pamela Tucker have my library card. I want to tell Miss Perone."

"That's very nice," Isabella said, "but it would be better for her to get her own."

"Her daddy won't let her."

So Isabella found the number. We thought it would be in the yellow pages, but it turned out to be in the government pages. Miss Perone said the same thing as Isabella. "It would be easy for her to get her own, and you know, you would be responsible for anything she — "

"Her daddy won't let her," I said. "He thinks the library's not for people like her or something."

"Okay," Miss Perone said. "I think we can work something out."

That phone call left me feeling so much better I wanted to call somebody else. I didn't feel like listening to Caroline. I looked through my desk for the blue slip of paper I'd brought home from Scout camp. It had Callie Thompson's number on it; I'd never called her before.

"You going to do Scouts next year?" I said.

"I hope so," she said, "but my choir practice might be on the same day."

"You worked on any more badges?"

"I can get dance now," she said.

"I can do the twist," I said.

"That's not a real dance." Callie Thompson didn't like to joke about badges.

"I haven't done much," I said. "I've been sick."

"From what?"

"Mumps."

"Oh," Callie said. "You better be careful. You can go deaf from that."

"Not from the mumps. They're not anything."

"Not for most people," Callie said, "but sometimes there are complications. You got to be careful of complications."

"Well," I said. "I just got the regular kind."

"Keep your head elevated so the poison doesn't drain into your ears."

"Okay, Callie."

"And you know what," she said. "You might be able to turn being sick into something for the first-aid badge." She thought about it. "You should get that one."

I laughed, but I was sure that Callie Thompson wasn't even cracking a smile.

Eighteen

Uncle Carter sold all the back acres at the homeplace. Aunt Celeste was mad. "Who does he think he is?" She tapped a cigarette on the kitchen counter. Mama pulled it out of her hand. "He didn't ask me. Did he ask you?"

"Well, he had to ask Mama," Mama said. "It's her name on the deed."

Aunt Celeste waved her arms around. "Don't you care?"

Mama leaned on the counter. She yawned. "About what?"

"About the homeplace. We grew up there, Bobbie."

"Tell me, Celeste," Mama said. "Would your pain be eased by a piece of the money he got for it?"

"It might."

"You see," Mama said, "you and me, we got a completely different view of this thing. Carter's lived with

Mama every day for almost forty years. He farmed that place full-time until he started getting all that overtime at the mill. As far as I'm concerned, he's earned it, and he's welcome to it."

"Well, Bobbie, that's just plain stupid. Don't you know about the way things are supposed to be shared equally, about inheritance, about — "

"Inheritance?" Mama said. "Did somebody die that I didn't hear about?"

"You know what I mean."

"Celeste, people like us don't have inheritances. People like us make our own way. Whoever Mama's not mad at when she dies, whoever's got the churn and the punch bowl in their house, that's going to be our inheritance."

"I don't see it that way."

"And now the poor boy's living out there with Macy and Mama? I say he's earned whatever he can get."

Daddy came out of the bathroom and said, "Bobbie?"

Mama pushed up off her stool. "Celeste, you got to either go home or sleep on our couch." She walked out of the kitchen without even seeing which Aunt Celeste was going to do. She saw me standing in the corner. "What are you doing out here?"

"Listening," I said.

"Well," Mama said, "show's over. Go to bed."

Daddy and Mama went into their bedroom. I

watched Aunt Celeste light a cigarette. She waved to me. I waved back and went to bed.

After we dropped Isabella off on Thursday, we picked Aunt Celeste up at Compton's. "So you think he's going to come clean?"

"He just said he had a surprise."

"How'd he sound?"

"Excited. Like a kid."

"Maybe Carter's bought himself a sports car," Aunt Celeste said.

"Yeah, right."

"I'm bringing it up," Aunt Celeste said. "About the money."

Mama groaned. We had to wait for a big truck to pull out of the driveway before we could turn in and park. Mama got out of the car. "What on earth — "

Uncle Carter walked up and said, "It's a double-wide."

"What are you doing with it?" Aunt Celeste said.

I had to stop Jesse from tumbling out of the car after me. He could one way or another get anywhere he wanted to go these days. Macy pulled in behind us. Grandma Graham hurried down the front-porch steps. Everyone's mouth was dropped open in surprise, except for Uncle Carter's. He grinned a big grin and motioned for us all to follow him.

"Notice," Uncle Carter said, "that all the furniture, all the fixtures, they're full-size, not that trailer-size, cut-down stuff."

145

Macy closed her mouth and took Uncle Carter's arm. "It's a classy color." It was a sort of grayish blue. "You hardly notice it's a trailer."

"Well, this really is more of a mobile home," Uncle Carter said.

Mama helped Grandma Graham up the steps into the mobile home.

"You'll have to put in an extra step, Carter," Macy said. "Make it easier for Miss Graham."

"Oh," Grandma said, standing in the doorway. "I don't plan to visit all that much. I'll leave that up to you young folks."

Macy looked at Uncle Carter. Her mouth was open again.

"You all will have to come on over, and we'll do our visiting in the house," Grandma said. Mama gave her her hand to help her down the steps. "You ought to take a look at that kitchen, Macy. You're going to love it."

"Carter?" Macy said. Her hand was off his arm.

Mama and Aunt Celeste raised their eyebrows at each other. Mama scooped up Jesse. "Well, it's real nice, Carter," she said. "I've got to get these kids home, but I'll be talking to you tomorrow."

At first Mama and Aunt Celeste didn't say anything to each other. They just shook their heads. Finally Mama said, "Well now, maybe you could get a piece of the action by moving into the trailer, or there's bound to be plenty of extra room in the house."

"No, thank you," Aunt Celeste said. "What do you think Carter's plan is exactly?"

Mama laughed. "I don't think it much matters." They laughed the rest of the way home.

That night Daddy's laughter woke me up. "Well, don't you see, Bobbie, he didn't ever have a plan. He's just throwing a bone at a couple of hungry dogs."

"Fred! That's my mother you're talking about."

"No, I'm talking about your brother. He might be one spineless shadow of a man, but he's smart."

"Well, I tell you, Mama never for a minute considered she was supposed to be moving into that trailer."

"If I'd known about it beforehand, and if I was a betting man," Daddy said, "I'd have put every nickel I had on Miss Graham."

There were three weeks until school started. The FOR RENT sign was still up in front of the white house. I spent a lot of time in the afternoons, when it was too hot for even Isabella to think I should be outside, practicing the duet in the back of the music book. Pamela Tucker was gone, and so I wasn't ever going to play it properly, with two people, but I practiced it anyway, until I knew it by heart.

There were two weeks left to my birthday. I was going to be eleven. "What do you want?" Mama asked me. I didn't know yet.

Jesse could pull himself up at the coffee table and

walk around it now. He said, "Raaa," and he meant me.

The days were long. "Maybe you should invite one of your friends over, maybe Caroline," Isabella said.

I shook my head and picked up the phone to call Callie Thompson instead. Might as well let her know I hadn't gone deaf. "What are you doing?"

"Arithmetic," she said.

"Arithmetic?" I said. "What for?"

"Review," she said. "School's starting."

"In three weeks."

"You forget a lot over the summer."

"I guess."

"You do," she said. "Get a pencil. Try this."

"I don't want to," I said, but I pulled over the pad and pencil because there was no getting out of it.

"Four hundred and seventy times twenty-six," she said.

I wrote it down. "Times?" I said.

"Times," she said. "Now think."

I couldn't believe this. "Three thousand seven hundred and sixty."

"Not even close." She sounded delighted. "Twelve thousand two hundred and twenty."

"Oh."

"When you multiply by the two in twenty-six, what is the two?"

"Two?"

"No, two tens."

148

"Oh yeah." It came back to me, about multiplying by two-digit numbers and adding the zero to mark the place and all that. "I just forgot." Callie made me do another problem just to be sure.

"You going to be a teacher when you grow up?" I said.

"No," she said. "A lawyer. What are you going to be?"

I didn't know. "I want to be famous," I said. "And live in a big city."

"That's not anything."

"A movie star then."

"That's stupid," she said.

"I don't really want to be a movie star," I said. "I just had a friend who wanted to be one." I didn't mean to do it, but all of a sudden I told Callie the whole story of Pamela Tucker, how it wasn't until she disappeared out my window I realized she was my secret and certain best friend, but I didn't even think I liked her before that.

"Well, what are you," Callie said, without thinking about it even for a little bit, "going to do about it?"

"What can I do?"

"You got this friend that just showed up one day on your front porch."

"Yeah?"

"Well, you can't be lucky all the time. Sometimes you got to do something yourself."

The way the phone rang, at the very moment I hung

up with Callie, I knew that Mama'd been trying to call for a while. "Who's been on the phone?"

"Me."

"We're busy." She sounded out of breath. "I'm going to drive by with some groceries, but I don't have time to get out, so you wait out front for me."

It was so hot by then that nobody was on the street, but Mama pulled up in front in about five minutes. I took out two bags of groceries and a carton of Cokes. "Got to run," she said. "Got to go by the bank."

Isabella came out to help me, but as soon as she picked up the carton of Cokes the bottom fell out of it. One of the bottles broke and a big chunk of glass bounced up into Isabella's leg. There was a lot of blood. She sat down on the step to take a look at it; I ran into the house for a cloth. She pressed it against the cut, soaking it with blood for several minutes before pulling it away. It was a bad, wide cut. "Isabella!" I said. "You're white!" The dark skin continued just a little way inside the cut, then the skin was white.

Isabella laughed. "What did you think? That I was black to the bone?"

"Well," I said. "Yeah."

Nineteen

What I wanted to do on my birthday was go for a ride on the city bus all by myself. I listened to Mama tell me again how when she was thirteen years old, she had gotten off a bus and been chased by a strange man, how she'd been wearing high heels even though she was too young to be wearing them, how she'd broken the heel off one and lost the other one right off her foot from running so hard. She'd gotten away, but she wasn't ever going to forget it.

I listened, but I didn't understand any more than I ever had what it had to do with me. "I'll be careful," I said. "It'll be in the daytime."

Mama couldn't bring herself to give me a straight answer, but I heard her bring it up with Daddy the night before my birthday. "I don't know," he said. "Where does she want to go?"

"I don't know," Mama said. "Into town, I would imagine."

I didn't know either.

151

"She's old enough," Daddy said. "Count your blessings. She could be wanting you to put on a party."

I would never want a birthday party. I had fun at Christmas parties and Halloween parties, but at birthday parties someone was always mad or hurt or sick or left out. The idea of being in the middle of one of my own scared me.

The next morning Isabella gave me a book of poems. It wasn't wrapped; she thought wrapping things in paper was wasteful and unnecessary. It was just like a book she had checked out for herself at the library a few times. After I had cried, after I had told her Pamela Tucker called her a nigger maid, she'd brought in that book and read me a poem about how the writer had been called "nigger" for the first time in Baltimore, Maryland, and how it felt.

Mama gave me a shorts set for me and a red two-piece suit for Barbie. She said Grandma Graham and Aunt Celeste would drop by a little later on in the evening to give me some presents and have some cake. Daddy gave me two dimes and two nickels for bus fare and three dollars to spend in town on anything I wanted. After my cornflakes and juice, Isabella and Jesse came out on the porch and watched me walk down to the corner where the bus stopped.

When Isabella and I had ridden the bus together, I was always talking, never looking where I was going. Today I wanted to look, but I'd sat in the wrong kind of seat — the kind that faced into the bus instead of straight ahead — so I had to turn around to look out the window. That wasn't comfortable.

It didn't take long to get to the town square. Anyone that was left by that time got off. Two people got on. The bus just sat and sat and sat.

"Did you miss your stop?" Howard asked.

I shook my head.

"Do you need a transfer?"

"Oh no, sir." Isabella had told me about transfers. Those would get me on other buses and take me too far.

"Well, then, where did you want to go?"

I still didn't know. "It's my birthday — "

"Well," he said and smiled.

"I'm eleven today, and I just wanted to take a bus ride, by myself, but I'm not really sure yet — "

His smile stretched even wider. "Well, I see, you're just getting the lay of the land, taking a trial run. I think that's real smart."

I smiled.

"Who are your folks?"

"Fred and Bobbie — " I didn't even have to get to our last name.

"You're Fred's little girl?" he said. "I know your mama and daddy real well. I stop in at Fred's nearly every day."

That didn't surprise me. Everybody I'd ever met knew Mama and Daddy and the store.

People began to climb on in clusters. The line of buses around the square hummed louder. Howard sat up straight and put both hands on the wheel. I slipped into the next seat that faced straight ahead so I could see better. In the distance I saw Dickersons' Ice Cream Shop.

There was James B. Dean's for Music — Aunt Celeste said they had listening booths in there, so you could listen before shelling out your money — and Sears. After the library it was mostly trees and houses, a few gas stations. I could see Brown Street coming up. Howard stopped even though I didn't pull the cord and looked around at me.

"Can I keep riding in the other direction?" I asked. "I've got another fifteen cents."

"Long as you don't get off, we're square," Howard said. He took his hand off the lever that opened the door and put it back on the big, flat steering wheel.

The trees began to have signs nailed on them. Houses became unpainted. The outside was ragged. The bus passed the back side of the Hard Road. Howard looked at me in his mirror and said, "Want to get off and visit your daddy?"

"No sir."

He smiled at me in his mirror. Sitting up high like I was in the bus, looking down the Hard Road hill, I could see Miss Hattie's roof had a hole in it next to the chimney.

154

"Never used to pass by here without picking up a crowd," Howard said. "But all the young'uns are gone now."

The trees, bushes, tall flowers and colored houses brightened up the street like balloons. Back in there somewhere was Chinaberry Lane. There were only two cars parked in front of my school.

"This used to be the last stop," Howard said. "But with this new subdivision going up they've extended the line a couple of blocks."

"What's that, sir?" I said. "A subdivision?"

"Oh, that's when they come in and bulldoze through a pasture or woods, and put up a whole lot of houses, and then everybody moves in, all at one time." He shook his head trying to explain it.

I'd never heard of such a thing. The bus turned into a dirt road. Four of the houses were finished, there was a car in one of the driveways. We passed what looked like a hundred house skeletons. There was a fancy wooden sign saying Laurel Lane. Passing back by the Hard Road was like moving through an ugly blotch left by a leaky fountain pen. It felt like a mistake. I could see why Jeannette and Tamara and Johnny Chastain went away. I hated passing by and leaving Daddy and Miss Hattie in there.

The bus came up on Brown Street, and Howard turned around and looked at me.

I shook my head. "I know where I want to go

now." I settled back and waited until the bus stopped again at the town square. "Thank you," I said to Howard when I got off the bus.

"It's very wise," he said, "to take your time with decisions."

I walked across the street and down beside the shoe store to Dickersons' Ice Cream Shop. There was a man having coffee at the counter and two teenagers eating French fries at the very back booth. The lady behind the counter was blond. Her hair was up in a French twist like Aunt Celeste was always trying to do; she could never get the front quite right. She was looking at me, so I sat down at the counter.

"What can I get you?" she said.

"French fries," I said. "And a Coke."

She set up the Coke and dropped an order of fries in the fryer. Then the front door swung open and in walked Pamela Tucker.

"Hey," I said.

"Hey," she said. She went behind the counter, tied her apron in front, then twisted it to the back, had a few words with the blond lady, then turned around and smiled at me.

Twenty

Mama bought me a plaid skirt to wear on the first day of school. The good thing about plaid, she said, was it would go with anything. I wore it with a red blouse that I already had.

There were two sixth grades. Callie Thompson and Cynthia were in my room, but Caroline was in the other one. At recess, when we were all together, Caroline told me that she was supposed to be in our room, but that our teacher, Miss Camp, had heard that it would be better for Cynthia and Caroline to be separated. They bickered so much.

I just nodded. I was with Miss Camp on that one. Caroline never said for sure how she felt about it, but as far as I could tell she liked being singled out like that.

Miss Camp gave us an assignment right away. It was a fun one. What if all of a sudden, she said, we could up and move anywhere we wanted to in the world? Where would that be? And why? New York popped into my head first thing, but I thought that might be too common, so I decided to look into another famous city, maybe one in another country. That afternoon Isabella, Jesse and I went to the library so I could find some books and get some ideas.

"I didn't get my card back from Pamela Tucker," I said. "If I have to, can I check out books on your card?"

"Of course," Isabella said.

I knew she would let me. She was already using her card to check out little ABC and nursery rhyme books for Jesse. "Piano lessons start back up next Tuesday."

"That's good," Isabella said.

"I told Pamela Tucker she could come over same as always. She could ride the bus."

"It would be good to see her."

I didn't have to worry about my card. Miss Perone gave it back to me as soon as I walked in. "Did she use it?" I asked.

"She did indeed."

"What did she check out?"

"She can tell you that herself," Miss Perone said. "But at any rate, thanks to you, she has her own card now."

"Did her daddy — ?"

Miss Perone shook her head. "We worked it out."

I sat in the geography aisle and looked and thought, but when it was time to go I still couldn't decide between Athens, Greece, Paris, France and Berlin, Germany. I checked out books on all of them, and later on that night, remembering the pretty sound of Miss Perone's French songs, I picked Paris.

The Sunday before the report was due — we had to give it out loud, in front of the whole class — Mama took it into her head to give me a permanent. "It'll give it some body," Mama said. I guess she didn't want to bring up getting it cut again. I had no idea it would turn out so curly, but pulled back on top with a barrette, it looked okay. Still, you didn't want everybody to stare at you and know right off that you'd done something different to yourself. It didn't help at all, having to stand up in front of the class and talk about Paris with twice as much hair as you'd had the week before.

"Your mama give you a permanent?" Cynthia asked. "Or did you go to a beauty shop?"

Caroline giggled. "Rachel caught a bad case of kinky hair at camp this summer."

I wasn't the only one that looked over at Callie Thompson, swinging by herself across the monkey bars, but I was the only one that went over, jumped up and followed behind her.

"I was just joking," Caroline said, when we were going back inside.

I shrugged. Caroline didn't want me to be mad, and I wanted her to say something to get me over it, but there wasn't any one thing she could say. It was more than that.

Miss Love came the next Tuesday and brought me a new book of songs. We worked on the first one for the hour, then I walked her to her car.

"Where's your little friend who used to wait outside?"

"I don't know." I could've explained to her about Pamela moving away and all, but I had expected her to be there, too.

It was three weeks before she came, and then it wasn't even on a Tuesday. It was the day after my music lesson, on a Wednesday. "I've been busy," she said. "I got school and work, and we're living all the way across town now."

Isabella hugged her. Jesse said, "Hi!"

"Wow," Pamela said.

"He says that to everybody," I said.

She'd found some magazines in the library with the music to popular songs printed up in the back. She opened up one to "Moon River." This blond girl, a year ahead of me, had sung it at the school talent show last year, and I didn't care for it too much, but it sounded better when Pamela played it. She used the pedals.

She opened up another one that had "Catch a Falling Star." I tried to follow the music while she played. "You're playing extra notes."

"Doesn't it sound right?"

"Yeah," I said. "It's just more than's on the page."

"I'm just filling in," she said. "Those notes go with those notes."

I nodded and took my turn trying to play it the simple way, the way it was on the page, the only way I could. A street sound built up, like a fly trapped between the window glass and the screen, without us taking much notice. Isabella, holding Jesse on her hip, ran past us, to see what it was.

Pamela and I followed her out on the front porch. Other people were gathered on the street. "Lord a mercy!" They were all looking up. "Look at that!" They were loud. Isabella went in to call Mama, but she couldn't get through. Sirens sounded. The black sky was spreading and beginning to smell. Pamela Tucker had to catch the bus back to her house anyway, so we walked down to the bus stop with her.

It was Howard that told us for sure what I already knew. The Hard Road and everything on it was burning down. "I saw your mama and daddy," he told me, "standing outside, safe and sound."

It took them about an hour to get home. "It's gone." That's all that Daddy said. He sat out on the back steps, smoking a cigarette.

"Is it bad? Is the store — ?"

Mama shook her head. "Everything's gone. Miss Hattie's dead," Mama said, "and you know that friend of hers — "

"Miss Edna?"

"That's it. She was visiting."

"Was Jeannette or Tamara or — "

Mama shook her head, "Just Miss Hattie and Miss Edna. They think it might have started there, in the fireplace."

Mama had Aunt Celeste make up chrysanthemum casket blankets for Miss Hattie and for Miss Edna, even though Miss Edna lived over in Harden Homes, and Mama didn't know her so well. "Those poor old women," Mama said. "They never had a chance."

I wanted to go to the funeral, but Mama didn't feel up to it. "I'll see Jeannette and Tamara," I said.

Mama shook her head. "It's not an occasion for visiting your friends."

I wasn't thinking about just visiting. I was thinking more about never ever seeing them again, about saying good-bye once and for all. On the day of the funeral Isabella and I walked down to the Hard Road and left a coffee can full of chrysanthemums — Miss Peaks let us pick them out of her yard — where Miss Hattie's house had been. All that was left was the chimney, and it was falling apart.

We looked around where the store had been, but Daddy was right; everything that was left he'd loaded into the pickup and brought home. There was a bread rack, one refrigeration unit and a couple of boxes of

162

loose brackets and whatnot stacked on our side porch at home. That was it.

Daddy went to work driving a truck for a beer distributor. Mama stayed home. Money was tight. Nothing and nobody was where it was supposed to be.

The store and the Hard Road were gone all at once, but the way I lost Isabella, a little at a time, was worse. I didn't even mind at first, when she stopped coming on Saturdays; that had only been for half a day anyway. I hardly noticed when she wasn't there on Mondays and Wednesdays. And I liked thinking of her where she was, it was so Isabella-like, so sweet, taking the load off the two Miss Loves. I'd been in their house, so even if she wasn't there, I could see her, imagine her polishing the piano or straightening the cluttered bedroom where I'd waited for my recitals. But then I lost her on Tuesdays and Thursdays, to another family. With children. On Fridays I avoided her. I closed my door. I went to the library. One day a week wasn't enough, and it wasn't right.

I was mad. I was mad at Daddy for not taking care of us better, for letting the store burn down. I was mad at Mama because no matter how good she made it, baking cookies and baking bread and being there, it wouldn't last. I was mad at Isabella for washing that little girl's hair, and then having the nerve to come into our house and talk about it.

And I knew it was crazy, but most of all I was mad

at Jesse for just jumping on Isabella every time he saw her, as if she'd been there the day before, as if she was going to come back the next day. I was mad at him because I thought if he pitched a fit, Mama and Isabella would pay attention in a way they wouldn't to me. He was still too much of a baby to be of any use and to come through for me.

Twenty-One

I was going to be a witch. Caroline was going to be a cowgirl, and Cynthia was going to be a princess. Callie Thompson was going to a party at her church; she didn't hold with the idea of dressing up. That was all that popped into my head, the Halloween talk, when I came home, and Isabella asked what I'd done in school. I didn't tell her about it though. I told her I had a book to read for a book report, took my cookies and milk into my room and closed the door. I didn't open it again until Mama came back from wherever she'd been and asked me if I was coming with her to take Isabella home. I said no.

That night Pamela Tucker came to me. She was there in a window again, but this time it was the window of a car, a very long, white car. The scarf around her neck was bright purple and her hoops were bigger than any I'd ever seen. The dark windows were rolled down just enough for me to see her face. She was smiling a very small, Pamela Tucker–type smile. The car wouldn't come to an end, but just kept going and going, and through another open window Isabella was reaching out her hand, waving to me.

I woke up from this dream with tears in my eyes, and it took me forever to get back to sleep. I hadn't even gone out to tell Isabella good-bye that afternoon.

The next day I told Mama I needed to go to the library.

"On a Saturday?" she said.

"I've got a social studies report next week," I said. There was no book report and no social studies report, at least not anytime soon. I said a little prayer and promised not to lie after today, and I knew God would forgive me. I wasn't trying to hide anything bad from Mama, I just didn't know how to explain to her how I was feeling and what I had to do.

"Just be home by four," she said. Ever since I'd come back safe and sound from my birthday bus ride, Mama hadn't seemed to worry as much about buses.

Howard gave me a sort of surprised look when I asked him for a transfer and what bus I'd need to get to Henderson Street. "What you up to over there?"

"I'm meeting Isabella," I said.

Howard shook his head. He held tight to the transfer.

"The lady that goes to the library with me."

"Oh." Howard smiled. "Your maid."

I sighed and took the transfer.

"Take the Evergreen," he said. "Straight shot."

It wasn't until the Evergreen bus turned onto the Boulevard that I knew where I was for sure. That was the way Mama always went to take Isabella home, and I was so used to going this way that it was as familiar as brushing my teeth in the morning. Still, it was different getting off the bus and walking on Henderson Street rather than just driving through in a closed-up car. I guess I'd noticed before, but I'd never thought much about the fact that Isabella's house had a dirt yard. I knew the wide, friendly porch, though, where Isabella always turned around for one last wave.

It was Isabella's brother, the Reverend Harris, that came to the door.

"Hello, sir," I said. "I'm Rachel — "

"I know." Isabella's brother had a lot of hair and wore a very interesting suit. It looked like it was made out of just plain, everyday cotton, not special suit cloth. It was black, and the jacket didn't have a collar.

"Is Isabella home?"

He frowned. "Is there some trouble?"

"No sir," I said. "I just wanted to see Isabella, just for a minute." Reverend Harris's head didn't move. I felt like he wanted me to say something else. "As a friend," I said.

He nodded. "One moment."

Isabella came out in a hurry, banging the screen door, looking around out front. I could see the Reverend Harris behind the screen, looking disapproving. "Is everything all right?"

167

I nodded. "I came on the bus."

Isabella took my hand, and we sat down in the big swing together. She smiled. "As a friend, Gary said."

And I couldn't help it. I laid my head on her shoulder and cried and cried. I thought she might think I was crazy, or that I was lying again when I said there wasn't any trouble, but Isabella just kept her arms around me and pushed the swing slowly with her feet. "You know, Rachel," Isabella said. "Gary was right when he said your family wasn't my family, no matter how happy we were together." She hugged me closer. "Your mama and daddy, they did what they had to do, under the circumstances, and they did right by me." She looked down, but I didn't look up. "You know that, don't you?"

I didn't move my head one way or the other. I didn't care. My head was stuffed up, and it hurt.

She pushed us back and forth in the swing for a while without talking. I felt foolish, but I was grateful for not having to explain myself, for having Isabella know just exactly why I was there.

"It was a happy time," she finally said, "but it came easy to us, being friends like we are. I came in and visited with you every day, but it was my job, all at the same time." She smoothed the hair back out of my eyes. "You know how nice Pamela Tucker played that piano — "

I nodded. I couldn't just lay there, stupid forever, without saying anything.

"She didn't have a piano, wasn't about to have a piano, but she loved the idea of playing one, so she had to invite herself over and ask you." Isabella laughed. "And do you know how hard it was for Miss Pamela Tucker to ask anyone for anything?"

I couldn't help it. I laughed and lifted my head. "It was just that pure wanting to."

"Sometimes that pure wanting to, that's all we've got," Isabella said. "But it's the tight times, not the easy ones, that makes us stronger, better and more special friends."

She took me inside and had me hold a cold, wet cloth over my eyes to take down the swelling. "I didn't tell Mama I came here," I said. "Not for any reason, just because — "

"We'll worry about that later," Isabella said.

On the bus ride back home, I saw Dickersons' Ice Cream Shop. It was too late to stop in today, but it was good just knowing Pamela Tucker was there and knowing she wouldn't go away without letting me know. Some nights, when the moonlight and streetlights came together particularly bright, I looked out and expected to see her face in my window.

I called Callie Thompson on the phone when I got home. It surprised me that I knew her number; the only other numbers I'd ever learned by heart were Grandma Graham's and the store's. Callie wasn't there, but her mother said she'd have her call. "I'm so glad, Rachel," her mother said, "to have the opportunity to tell you how sorry I was to hear about your father's business. We all remember you in our prayers."

"Thank you, ma'am," I said. I'd never talked to her before, but she sounded as if she knew all about me. That made me feel good.

When Daddy came home from work on Monday, he didn't do the usual thing, which was say nothing, light up a cigarette and go sit by himself on the back steps. He said, "Get a jacket or whatever. We're going out to eat."

"I've got a meat loaf," Mama said.

"Save it," he said.

This was unusual, not just because money was supposed to be tight, but because going out to eat wasn't something we did even when money wasn't tight. I'd heard people at school talk about going to restaurants as a regular thing, but we always ate at home, except for grabbing a fish sandwich or a hot dog to eat in the car while we were on our way somewhere else.

"Where are we going?" Mama said when we were all packed in the car.

"Place called The Block."

I'd never heard of it.

Mama made a face. "You mean that place out on Twenty-nine?"

Daddy nodded.

The parking lot wasn't clean. I'd always thought Daddy was a little crazy about keeping the parking lot picked up around the store, but now I could see what could happen if you just let it go. The inside had that same look to it, not dirty, just not kept-up.

Daddy sat beside me in the booth. Mama put a blanket down on the other side and laid Jesse down — the car ride had put him to sleep — and slid in beside him. I checked out the menu on the table. "They have egg salad," I said.

"No," Daddy said. "Grilled cheese or hamburger. You'll probably want that meat loaf when we get home."

"Grilled cheese," I said.

Daddy nodded, leaned on his elbows and whispered to Mama, "First delivery I made here, well, I thought it was just a bad day." The waitress came over to take our order. "Grilled cheese and Cokes all round," Daddy said. "Those sandwiches come with chips?"

"That's extra." The waitress didn't crack a smile.

Daddy raised his eyebrows at Mama. "Bag of chips, then," he said. "Thanks." When she was gone he took up his whispering again. "Second and third time, I could see it was just the regular way of business around here."

There was a crash from the kitchen. "Watch what you're doing, you idiot!" somebody yelled. Jesse woke up, and Mama sat him in her lap and bounced him.

Daddy didn't even notice. "So I found out who owns this place, had a casual little talk with him, found out he's desperate for a new manager."

171

Mama's eyes brightened. She smiled. Jesse smiled at me, and I laughed.

Daddy leaned in closer. "The way I see it, I come in as manager, we really tighten our belts, try to put something away to go with the insurance money, and in about six months he'll be more than ready to let me take it off his hands."

Mama sat up straight. She nodded. She took a slow look around the room. I took it in, too. I knew what she was seeing — a bright, busy, perfect place like the store. We couldn't eat but half of those greasy sandwiches, but we sat in the booth for the better part of an hour, all filled up with that pure wanting to.